Transit Comet Eclipse

Muharem Bazdulj

TRANSIT COMET ECLIPSE

Translated from the Bosnian by Nataša Milas

DALKEY ARCHIVE PRESS

Originally published in Bosnian by Ajfelov Most as *Tranzit, kometa, pomračenje* in 2007.

Library of Congress Cataloging-in-Publication Data
Names: Bazdulj, Muharem, 1977- author. | Milas, Natasa, translator.
Title: Transit, comet, eclipse / Muharem Bazdulj ; translated by Natasa Milas.
Other titles: Tranzit, kometa, pomraécenje. English
Description: First Dalkey Archive edition. | Victoria, TX : Dalkey Archive Press, 2018. | "Originally published in Bosnian by Ajfelov Most as *Tranzit, kometa, pomraécenje* in 2007" -- Verso title page.
Identifiers: LCCN 2017035409 | ISBN 9781628972382 (pbk. : alk. paper)
Subjects: LCSH: Yugoslavia--History--Fiction. | Psychological fiction.
Classification: LCC PG1745.B39 T7313 2018 | DDC 891.8/3936--dc23
LC record available at https://lccn.loc.gov/2017035409

www.dalkeyarchive.com
Victoria, TX / McLean, IL / Dublin

Co-funded by the Creative Europe Programme of the European Union

Dalkey Archive Press publications are, in part, made possible through the support of the University of Houston-Victoria and its programs in creative writing, publishing, and translation.

Printed on permanent/durable acid-free paper

Astrology furnishes a splendid proof of the contemptible subjectivity of men. It refers the course of celestial bodies to the miserable ego: it establishes a connection between the comets in heaven and squabbles and rascalities on earth.

Arthur Schopenhauer

Looking up at the stars, I know quite well
That, for all they care, I can go to hell

W. H. Auden

And of the threads that connect the stars and of wombs
And of the father-stuff

Walt Whitman

Transit

People in the East live in a roundabout way. What matters to them is not getting ahead but the way of life, what is said along the way, or the name given to the regions one traverses.

Ivo Andrić: *Signs by the Roadside*

I

ON THE SIXTH OF June, 1762, sometime in the afternoon, Daniel Danon was approached by a rather odd fellow at the Karnobat fair. There were various sorts of people at the famous Karnobat fairs and Daniel, a mirror merchant from Istanbul, had seen numerous wonders in his day. Still, the foreigner managed to surprise him. He was about fifty years old. His hair was thick, black, and coarse; his eyes deeply set; his nose aquiline and rather large; his lips thin and dark, as if they were hiding a restrained sensibility; his look intelligent and distrustful. The foreigner was tall, self-confident, almost arrogant. He was looking at Daniel's mirrors, observing them, circling around them. The foreigner didn't seem to mind the noise at the fair; he didn't even notice it. He finally lifted his eyes, looked at Daniel's face and spoke. It was barely noticeable but a smile played on the corner of Daniel's lips. He understood the foreigner. Daniel moved through the Balkans, from Belgrade to Izmir, from Travnik to Thessalonica, he was exposed to Slavic words and he himself used them. True, the foreigner's speech seemed a little different, it sounded archaic, but they understood each other nevertheless. The foreigner asked Daniel where he had acquired his mirrors, he mentioned the names of craftsmen and towns, he spoke about mercury and lead. Daniel's responses were brief and cautious. He gestured more than he spoke. What could he even say to this foreigner who clearly knew more about mirrors than he did. This type of man doesn't hang mirrors on the wall; he needs them for different purposes. Soon the foreigner stopped talking about mirrors and instead asked Daniel about the town of Karnobat itself. What devil was this foreigner, as if he knew that Daniel's mother was from Karnobat and that he actually knew a thing or two about the town. The foreigner inquired about the number of Turkish and Christian houses, he wanted to know whether there were any Jews in town, when they had moved there, who their rabbi was, and whether they were schooled. Daniel responded briefly, with uncertainty. The foreigner nodded. He further inquired from Daniel about the fair, about the sheep, and the distance to Markely Fortress. Thank you, said the foreigner at the end. He turned his back on Daniel and left. Daniel's eyes followed him. The foreigner walked away sure-footedly. He made no more stops; not by the merchants selling soap and candlesticks, nor by the butcher's—though the aroma of onion sausage was tempting—and not even by the tables with wool and clothing. It was hot. Daniel wiped the sweat off his forehead and thought how by the look of things this foreigner didn't even mind the heat. Daniel's eyes followed him until the last trace of the foreigner's cloak was out of sight. What a peculiar priest, Daniel muttered quietly.

The foreigner was actually a Jesuit. His name was Ruđer Bošković. He was traveling through Karnobat on his way from Istanbul to Petrograd. He traveled in a company that was even stranger than he. It was because of Bošković that they had stopped in Karnobat. He was interested in the town, in the fair, he was interested in everything. While he was making his way back to his fellow travelers, he was trying to remember everything of importance that he had heard and seen. To remember, at least before writing it down. They had been traveling for fourteen days. Bošković had already written about Kanara (a Christian village, about fifty houses), Fakia (a Christian village, eighty-eight houses), Karabunar (a town with six hundred houses, Turkish and Christian), and Harmanli (a Tatar village). In Karnobat, there were Jews as well. As his impressions settled his step quickened. I've seen what I needed to see here, now it's time to continue the journey. The crowded fair remained behind. He approached the resort where the Ambassador Porter and his retinue waited for him.

James Porter had been the English ambassador in Istanbul for more than fifteen years. I find Istanbul even more beautiful than London, he used to say to his friends. He decided, nevertheless, to return to his homeland. In King James's Bible, he remarked once to Bošković, it is written that the good Lord gave us seventy years of life, or more precisely, as it is clearly noted, sixty years and ten. In the first ten years we are not aware that we are alive. I spent a quarter of the Lord's remaining sixty years among the Turks. It's time to go back, Porter said. Bošković listened to him carefully but he knew that his decision had nothing to do with the Bible, nostalgia, or with metaphysics. Porter was going back to England because that is what his wife wanted. Porter would not stay in his homeland more than a few months, Bošković was convinced, Mistress Porter would find a way for them to be closer to her homeland. Beatrice Porter couldn't even try to hide her love for her native Holland. Bošković had nothing against loving one's homeland, even though it was easier for him to imagine love for a town or village than for a whole country, but this love of homeland had to have some limits. Love for one's country shouldn't justify a lie. My native Dubrovnik is very dear to me, but the truth is even dearer, Bošković would say. For Beatrice Porter lies were allowed when expressing one's patriotism. Maybe not lies exactly but pure ignorance. Bošković could not keep quiet about it any longer. He had been grateful to Ambassador Porter for his invitation to travel with them, but gratitude for him wasn't equal to subdued humility. Beatrice and Bošković quarreled. Even when their misunderstanding was smoothed over, Bošković realized that the ambassador's wife did not particularly favor him.

The whole affair began very innocently. It was the thirty-first of May. They had traveled together for a week. Around their unusual caravan there was an atmosphere of harmony and mutual warmth. In the early afternoon they made a stop by a rather small clearing to take a rest. Beatrice remained with her children while Bošković and Porter talked about London. After ten minutes of conversation they suddenly fell silent, but they were not good enough friends to find the silence comfortable. Bošković gazed around the clearing. Only then did he seem to notice a multitude of very beautiful and luxuriously multicolored tulips. Nowhere are tulips as lovely as in Turkey, he said only to break the silence. At that moment Beatrice appeared. The most beautiful tulips are in my country, she said. Bošković shrugged. Everyone finds the flowers of their homeland beautiful, he thought. Tulips are Dutch flowers, she said, and turned toward her children. Not true, the Jesuit raised his voice, tulips are Eastern flowers. Beatrice stopped and stared at Bošković. Tulip is a Persian word and it comes from the word turban. Before it blossoms, the tulip, as you know, resembles a turban. Turks call it *lala*, and that's what it is also called where I am from. The Turks value tulips, the ambassador carefully entered the conversation, they even call the period at the beginning of this century the "Epoch of Tulips." All of Istanbul was mad about tulips. They would pay for their bulbs with gold. The woman interrupted him: that was in Holland! It had been like that in Holland as well, true, Bošković began again, but a century earlier. In your country at that time, Madame, people would pay even a thousand forints for one bulb. That, however, has nothing to do with the origin of the flower. The good Lord wanted tulips to blossom in the Orient. They only reached Europe, and your country, sometime in the sixteenth century. This happened thanks to one very interesting man— Augerus Gislenius Busbequius, the illegitimate son of a French nobleman. Busbequius was the ambassador in Istanbul, serving Ferdinand the First two centuries before your respected husband. He sent the first tulip bulbs to your homeland, but that is a long story. It's time to get going, the ambassador used this moment to interrupt. We haven't the time for long stories. It was a pleasure to listen to you, Porter said to Bošković. Yes it was, Beatrice added, it is agreeable to hear things that remind you of your homeland.

Porter did not like long stops on a journey. He was in a hurry. This trip is long and difficult enough on its own, he said, I will not prolong it with needless stops. Night is for rest, he said. To tell the truth, Porter made the trip more difficult for himself. The ambassador couldn't stand traveling by sea. He suffered from chronic seasickness with very severe symptoms. In youth he used to hide this fact, thought of excuses and justifications, but he didn't wish to do that any longer. He was at an age now when he no longer felt like lying about it. He couldn't even imagine trying to stand all those humiliating dizzy spells and unbearable fits of nausea and vomiting. I'll go by land, come what may, he decided. The war between England and Austria was an additional problem. The war was why Porter couldn't travel on the usual, shorter route through Hungary and Vienna. He would have to travel, then, through Bulgaria, Moldova, and Poland, with his wife and children for that matter. A number of diplomats also accompanied them on the journey, along with the Greek nurse Lily and the servants. Porter knew that Bošković was traveling to Petrograd so he invited him to travel with them for part of the way. We have one big and one small carriage, as well as a carriage for luggage, you won't be uncomfortable, said the ambassador. We'll be honored to be in the company of such an erudite man. Bošković, naturally, agreed. The Jesuit spent seven months in Istanbul, which dragged on, he used to say, like seven years. He had traveled to Istanbul to observe the transit of Venus over the Sun. During his journey he made an unforeseen long stop in Italy and tried to observe the transit from Venice. It was cloudy. He couldn't see anything and became quite alarmed. The next transit of Venus over the Sun would take place in eight years, and by then, who knows if he'd be alive. The irony lies in the fact that eight years is such a short interval for Venus and the Sun. After the eight-year interval, the transit after that one wouldn't happen for at least a century. Bošković set out for Istanbul from Venice. On his journey he saw the ruins of the ancient city of Troy. He arrived in Istanbul in late autumn. As soon as they met, Porter told him that he watched the transit from Istanbul, where the visibility had been excellent. Bošković had met many ambassadors in his day but this Porter was a rare example of a pleasant one. At this point he would even have agreed to travel with unpleasant ambassadors. He had grown tired of Istanbul, he was in a hurry to get to Russia, but the roads were unsafe even for Muslims, let alone for Catholics. The diplomatic caravans were escorted, which made this situation almost ideal. He looked forward to a comfortable carriage. Within his first few days in Istanbul he sprained his ankle and walked with difficulty after that for almost two months. His leg stopped aching at times, except when the weather would change. Bošković nevertheless feared that there was something really wrong with it. He didn't have trouble walking but he feared the pain.

When he saw the horses and the carriages, the Jesuit slowed down his pace. I am getting close, he thought, now I can slow down. Soon enough he saw Porter, who was clearly becoming anxious. Porter noticed him as well. Hurry up, he called, it's time, we've been waiting for a while. Bošković unwillingly sped up.

Have you seen something new, Beatrice asked acerbically, as if such a learned man could learn anything new. Man learns all his life, Bošković responded briefly. The coachman clucked to the horses and the creaking wheels slowly started moving.

The road was flat, the landscape monotonous, and Bošković dozed off. In the past few years it was easier for him to fall asleep in the afternoon than at night. He thought about his Dubrovnik childhood, deserted city streets during the scorching heat, and the siesta when only the children were awake. His mother Pavica liked to sleep after lunch, just after noon. She rarely slept longer than an hour but she used to say that this one hour of sleep was dearer to her than five hours at night. Mother must be asleep now too, Bošković thought. He stirred a bit. His thigh was throbbing. He couldn't tell if this was the beginning of pain or just fear that there might be pain. He recognized the source of that fear. Bošković only remembered his father as an invalid and he thought about his father's paralyzed lower limbs. Bošković had no pain in his legs. He felt as if he had no legs at all. Even pain is better than nothing, that sounded familiar, he had read it somewhere, but couldn't remember where. His eyes were already closed. His thoughts and memories mixed almost imperceptibly with the fabric of shallow dreams, which aren't even real dreams when you know you're dreaming. The images of thirty minutes ago alternated with those from thirty years ago, the voices of the dead and those of his fellow travelers, the scent of the Adriatic Sea and the stink of London's fog. Less and less reality lingered in Bošković's senses, less and less consciousness. All structure was lost, the logic of dreams took over. The time and the place disappeared, the voices withered away. Only Porter's whisper could be heard, only a few words, only: hush, Father Bošković is sleeping, before he completely fell asleep.

II

On the tenth of June, in the late afternoon, almost before dusk, Ruđer Bošković sat at the square in Skalikavak and observed Gypsy musicians. They had planned to arrive in Skalikavak only by evening, but since they had taken only a brief break that day at lunchtime—and even then Porter rushed them—they made it to Skalikavak by daylight. In the midst of this settlement a rather large group of people gathered. Bošković was used to the fact that their caravan attracted attention, but he hadn't encountered such a crowd in the places they previously visited. Soon enough he realized that it was the Gypsies who were drawing the crowd and not they. The atmosphere was very carnival-like. People were merry. They drank and danced. These Gypsies were fine musicians. The lively melody made Bošković stomp his foot, the one that didn't hurt. The children liked the music the most. Little Anne Margaret began dancing herself. Even two-year-old Charles clapped his hands. Bošković rarely ever spent time in the company of small children. He was repelled by their irrationality and frailty, but he was very surprised by the warmth he had felt toward Anne Margaret over the past twenty days. The feeling was, so it seems, mutual. The little girl liked Bošković almost as much as her mother disliked him. Bošković had seen her before, two or three times in Istanbul, but it was only now during their trip that he paid her any attention. Or, more correctly, the girl paid attention to him and he responded. One morning, the little girl stared for a long time at Bošković's face. He could not ignore such an intelligent look. He addressed her, not knowing what to expect. The girl started talking in a more meaningful way than could be expected from a four-year-old. She asked him where he was from, if he had any family, and if he liked to travel. He caught himself responding to this little girl more openly and with more honesty than he would have done with an adult. In the following days he told her the names of trees and birds, about his childhood and his travels, he told her stories. Now he was looking at her dance, unaware that he was smiling. I never had children nor will I ever have any, he thought. This may be the only child to whom I mean something, if briefly.

Dusk stepped over the horizon. The evening was descending on them. People were parting. Soon a man from the retinue would approach Bošković and walk him to his lodgings. Bošković took a look around. He wanted to ask someone about Skalikavak, at least the main points, how many people lived there, how many of them were Christians, how many were Turks. A man appeared out of the dark, addressing Bošković in pure Italian. The Jesuit was surprised, especially once he realized who had approached him. This was a Gypsy man, old and corpulent, with a long, disheveled beard. My name is Melquiades, he said. Bošković quickly started the conversation, and soon he loosened up. Melquiades, it seemed, knew more languages than Bošković and traveled more than him, that is, if the Gypsy wasn't lying. There are two hundred and fifty houses in Skalikavak, he said, two hundred Bulgarian and fifty Turkish. As is rarely the case, he added, Bulgarians and Turks live together here in harmony. They even marry. They always receive us, the Gypsies, kindly even though it doesn't enter their minds to marry one of us, he mumbled through hoarse laughter.

The Gypsy disappeared a moment before Bošković was approached by a man from his retinue. The man took Bošković to a modest house where he was to spend the night. The Gypsy hadn't lied, Bošković discovered. His hosts were a Bulgarian man and his Turkish wife. The house was clean, the supper rich, the bed wide and soft. The Bulgarian understood Bošković's mother tongue and Bošković understood him as well. They chatted after dinner. Soon afterward Bošković retired for the night. He fell asleep quickly.

In the next few days the landscape was quite dreary. They traveled faster than they had over the previous days, which made Porter the happiest of all. If it weren't for the women and children he wouldn't even rest at night. The ambassador was one of those people who could imagine any type of misfortune and obstacles. The longer the journey the more dangerous it is, he had once said. Bošković responded with two words: *festina lente*. Bošković was inclined to attribute the ambassador's distaste for sea travel less to seasickness and more to Porter's need to keep everything under control. At sea, more than anywhere else, one needs to be ready for surprises, which ambassador Porter didn't like at all. This man may be an ideal diplomat, but he was definitely not an ideal traveling companion.

Once they arrived in Jenibazar, in the early afternoon, on the thirteenth of July, they talked Porter into making a stop there to rest until the next day. We still have six or seven hours until night, he said. He couldn't, however, ignore the fact that for two nights they had not slept in a bed. In fact, he couldn't refuse Beatrice. Despite their disagreements, this time Bošković was thankful to her. He had very personal reasons why he wanted to spend the night in this town.

The Ottomans called the town Jenibazar. The Bulgarians called it Novi Pazar. Another Novi Pazar, the city's namesake, larger and more to the west, closer to his native Dubrovnik, played a part in Bošković's family history. Bošković's father made most of his fortune precisely in Novi Pazar. He had lived there for years. The merchants from Dubrovnik held this town to be very important. Had his father remained any longer in Novi Pazar he would never have married and Bošković would never have been born, would never have existed. Bošković knew he was born of fire. Novi Pazar was burnt in one of the Turco-Austrian wars. That is when his father decided to go back to Dubrovnik. Upon his return he married Bošković's mother. They had six sons, he was the youngest, the youngest son of fire—as if in a fairy tale. This Novi Pazar was not the Novi Pazar, he knew that, but the name was a sign.

Jenibazar, Novi Pazar, had about three hundred houses: for each Bulgarian house there were five Turkish houses. There were also a few Vlach houses. Bošković happened to spend a night in one of these. This time the Slavic words of his childhood did not help him, the language of his host was more like Italian and French. The conversation with his host was rather exhausting despite the fact that they found ways to communicate. The host considered himself a Christian yet he didn't even know how to cross himself properly, let alone to say his Pater Noster. He was illiterate but very arrogant. He looked at Bošković condescendingly especially after he asked the man for the ways he expressed his faith. As if this Roman monk should teach me, me who preserved his faith here amongst the Ottomans, is what Bošković's host thought, or so Bošković thought.

The next day they traveled again without getting much rest. It was as if Porter wanted to make up for time he felt they'd lost. Bošković began to read Suetonius. *De Vita Caesarum* was his favorite read. He enjoyed books, which like a whirlpool drew him into his own world. On this June day, Julius Caesar, Octavius Augustus, and Tiberius were more alive to him than were ambassador James Porter, his wife Beatrice, and their two children all together. Once they arrived in the village where they were to spend the night Bošković neglected his earlier routine. He didn't seek a collocutor, nor did he inquire about the place. He waited quietly to be taken to the house where he was to spend the night. It turned out, however, that the host for the night was a village priest, an Orthodox one, for that matter. They understood each other using Slavic words. At one point Bošković unintentionally switched to Latin. The priest looked at him blankly. Bošković realized that the priest understood not a single word. He pulled out the book by Suetonius and laid it in front of the man. His host, Todor was his name, leafed through the pages with his greasy hands and just shrugged. Bošković wondered if this priest was even literate. The priest started asking Bošković about Rome, what kind of city that was, if there were any priests there, if there were any baptized folk. Bošković couldn't believe this, he thought that perhaps his host was making peculiar jokes. But this was not the pinnacle. After they had had a bit to drink the host leaned toward Bošković and in a whisper asked him what he had been punished for. Why punished? The Jesuit was puzzled. You have no beard, and that Englishman hasn't one either, he said in a barely audible voice. You must have committed some sin, a serious offence. Bošković tried to convince his host that both the ambassador and he shave their beards by choice, and that such a thing was common in Rome, London, and Paris, but his collocutor didn't seem to believe him. They parted and went to bed late that night. Todor was still dismissing what he had heard, thinking that the foreigner was hiding a major crime from him, in all likelihood some kind of conspiracy.

The following day they set off toward Baltchik. If we waste no time, Porter said, we could get there in three days. Not wasting time for Porter meant to be moving constantly while daylight lasted. It was the middle of June. These were the longest days in the year. Bošković was mainly reading. Time passed slowly. You know, he said to Porter, it is now clear to me why, when they speak of a long time period in my homeland, they say—a summer day until noon. Porter smiled sourly.

When they arrived in Baltchik the trouble had just begun. In Baltchik, in contrast to the other towns through which they passed, the Bulgarian and Turkish settlements were physically separated, almost as if they were two separate towns. They stopped in the Bulgarian part of the town. They were told not to worry: everything was all right there, they said. There was, however, the suspicion that the plague broke out among the Turks. Several people had abruptly died. Porter did not want to take risks. We need rest, he said, but safety matters more than comfort. They camped in the open air, in tents.

Porter, Beatrice, the nanny, and the rest of the retinue decided to enjoy themselves as if they were on an outing, as if the plague wasn't lurking, as if they weren't in the midst of the wild East and instead at some lakeshore in England. That's how they behaved. Everything was blue and green before their eyes. The sun shone as in a fairy tale. Bošković worried, he grumbled, he read. He missed the roof over his head, at least some modicum of comfort. He looked forward to his stay in Baltchik. This was a town about whose beauty Ovid had written, a poet who was exiled from his land by a tsar from his own book. Instead of resting and walking through the city, they were buffooning under the clear sky. Bošković was bothered by Porter's relaxed mood, more than by his previous hurriedness. He was bothered by the jokes, by the laughter. He went to bed right after the children while the rest of them played cards by the fire. That night Bošković couldn't sleep for a long time. In the morning, the children woke him up. Little Anne Margaret poked him with a twig and laughed. When he got up, all distracted and drowsy, he bumped into Beatrice. She laughed as if she had seen a vaudeville show. Grumpily he asked Porter if they were going to continue the journey today or waste more time. We are leaving right after breakfast, Porter answered, are you in a hurry now?

Porter tried to cheer him up once they got into the carriage. He talked about the experience of his fifteen years as a consul. Bošković had heard some of these stories before, but Porter was such a witty man, a true storyteller, which made it very pleasant to listen to him even when he spoke of things already known. We traveled through all of Bulgaria, Pater, only a few Europeans have done so. Tomorrow, I believe, we will reach the Danube.

The wind started blowing during the night. Bošković woke up often. The next day he expected to hear the murmur of the big river. The wind, however, slowed the horses. Bošković would, every now and then, mistake the loud wind for the sounds of the river. Sometime after noon the wind quieted down. They were soon able to hear a powerful roar. It was nothing like the wind. We are close, Porter said, the Danube can be heard. Wallachia is right over the river, he added, and after that comes Moldova, and that's where we are headed. Moldova, said Bošković in a half whisper. He had traversed all of Bulgaria, but the word "Bulgaria" never gave off anything mystical. He'd never been to Wallachia before, but he did not feel he was entering some unknown world either. But Moldova was something else. It sounded like a land from a story, from a legend, from a child's dreams. It sounded like a place from a book. Unreal. I'm going to Moldova, Bošković thought. He felt his heart beating somewhat faster. Was it from the beauty, or fear? The Danube was murky, the air foggy and gray, the other shore was not even visible.

III

Nothing was the same on the other side of the river. The land was different, perhaps softer, the air more moist, the heat heavier, barely tolerable. Bošković sweated. Porter still insisted on traveling faster, but the horses were tired. After they crossed the river they spent the night on an open plateau by the roadside. They hadn't yet seen a single settlement, a house, or a man there. The daybreak was murky. It was hot and stuffy with grayness in the air. It seemed as if the sky had lowered and the Sun was barely visible. Everyone was quiet and grumpy. The landscape was dreary. In the late afternoon, just before dusk, as Bošković was fearing spending yet another night on the ground, they saw the outline of several houses. The mood quickly livened. They soon arrived at the village. People approached the caravan timidly. When someone finally spoke, Bošković was struck by the unknown language. There was nothing familiar in its melody or in the vocabulary. Someone from the retinue happened to know the language so Porter was soon able, through the interpreter, to find them quarters for the night with several different hosts. Bošković's host was a young, taciturn man. It appeared that he and his wife had no children. Neither Latin nor Slavic words meant anything to this man. He responded only to pantomime. The man's name was Nicolas, as Bošković managed to learn. The place was called Galatz. The house was very small but pristine.

The next day they set off at earliest dawn. If we hurry we'll make it to Bauz before dark, Porter said. There is a monastery in Bauz where we can get a decent rest. It would be nice to stay at the monastery until dark. Tonight is Midsummer night. It would be lovely to dream a summer night's dream under the roof of a church, Beatrice muttered to herself, but loudly enough so the others could hear. Oh, Shakespeare, that English bard, the king of all poets, Bošković noted through a smile, looking at Beatrice. Did you know, said Bošković, that the bard mentions my birthplace in four of his plays: *Twelfth Night, Measure for Measure, The Merchant of Venice,* and *The Taming of the Shrew.* I didn't know, snorted Beatrice. Pater, you mentioned, as I recall, that in London you met Dr. Samuel Johnson, the ambassador said. Yes, said Bošković. I had the honor to discuss Shakespeare with him. I also had the privilege of talking with Arthur Murphy, who is considered by some to be the leading contemporary dramatist. I also met a very insightful young man by the name of Edmund Burke. Yes, so we have heard, said Beatrice. We also heard that Sir Joshua Reynolds painted your portrait, isn't that true? No Madame, replied Bošković. I had an opportunity to dine with Sir Reynolds once, but he did not paint my portrait. My great portrait was painted by Sir Robert Edge Pine at his own insistence. I'm not certain I've heard of him, Beatrice concluded, raising her eyebrows and turning to the window of the carriage. This renewed remembrance of the days Bošković had spent in London spurred Porter's nostalgia. For the umpteenth time he asked Bošković about his impressions of London, adding every now and then that they were not traveling fast enough. He is impatient, too impatient, Bošković thought, as if they were to arrive in London tonight and not in little Bauz.

They arrived at the monastery before dark. The church and the monastery were located outside of the town. It was there, in this monastery, that Bošković realized how much he missed Europe, missed home. He was not thinking about Dubrovnik, about Rome, Milan, Paris, London, yet at the same time he thought about all of these places and many others. He thought of home as a place of cleanliness, comfort, culture, and civilization. This monastery where he bathed, where he dined, where he conversed heartily, and where he was about to enjoy a night's rest, this monastery in comparison to the monasteries he had visited before seemed impoverished and dilapidated, but it was still part of that same world, the worse part of that world without a doubt, but a part nevertheless. Bulgaria seemed so dirty in comparison to this place. A piece of Old Europe, almost atavism, is how this monastery seemed. Yet, it still resembled the feral in the midst of a barbarian desert. The light will reach this country, Bošković thought as his consciousness slipped into the dark.

The night at the monastery—that Midsummer night—revived them all. It appeared that Midsummer night fires for a moment helped them see just how far they had traveled and how much still lay between them and home. Porter was relaxed, Beatrice in bright spirits, little Anne Margaret playful. In a few days we will be in Jassy, Porter said, and that is already a city, a real city. The initial enthusiasm from the beginning of the trip returned. Bošković went back to reading Suetonius. When he didn't read he talked to Porter or enjoyed the landscape. Moldova was beautiful: green forestland with burbling streams and powerful rivers, but deserted. They saw almost no one on the road. And even when they did, these rare people would keep off the road until the caravan passed. From fear, I suppose. These people are not used to strangers, Porter said. The fact that newcomers usually brought them misfortune makes it even worse, thought Bošković. There is nothing here in abundance but beauty and fear.

Moldovan nights seemed darker than anywhere else in the world. That's what it's like when it's deserted: neither moon nor stars can, by themselves, dispel the darkness. They were deeply quiet, the Moldovan summer nights. Thick black darkness and the heavy cloak of silence did not agree with Bošković's sleep. Thoughts tumbled in his head: from Suetonius's Roman Empire to concerns for his health and attention to his own inner personality. He looked forward to each dawn, he looked forward to the continuation of the journey, he became more impatient than Porter. Once we reach Jassy the more difficult part of our journey is over, he thought. That is anxiety for you, he thought. Jassy is beginning to look almost like a suburb of Petrograd. A long road is ahead of me, much of it without this diplomatic comfort. If only my leg doesn't start hurting again, he thought, and this thought seemed almost to bring on the pain.

On the twenty-eighth of June, before noon, Jassy appeared on the horizon. We made good time, Porter observed with pleasure. From Istanbul to Jassy in thirty-five days, yet everyone said it would take us at least forty. Thirty-five days, only five weeks, said Porter, while Bošković was thinking about the name of the town they were entering. This town was also mentioned somewhere by Ovid. The serpentine road was winding by the river between two hills. The city spread over the hills and the valley in between them.

Jassy was a city of wood. This was Bošković's first and strongest impression of the place. What stone was in other cities, in Jassy was wood. The city streets were not paved, or cobbled. They were made of wood, like floors, like the decks of ships, like bridges. Houses in Jassy were made of wood too. They weren't just modest huts. Jassy was a city of luxurious wooden houses, charming wooden facades, steep wooden roofs. The bed of the surreally blue river, which ran through the middle of the city, was wooden too. Like a city from a fairy tale, thought Bošković, remembering stories he had heard in childhood, as if it were a city on a ship floating on the sea.

We'll stay here for five days, said Porter. We'll spend five days in the summer residence of the Prince. The residence, a real wooden palace, was located by the riverbank. The river was called the Bahluiu, Bošković learned from the Prince's delegate who came to welcome them. The delegate spoke Italian. He was courteous and talkative. The Prince is particularly looking forward to seeing you, Pater, the delegate said to Bošković. He insisted that I tell you this. The Prince knows a great deal about you, he read some of your books, and he is so happy you have come to Jassy, said the deputy, and Bošković struggled between the flattery and his own skepticism. Could they have heard of me in this wooden fairy-tale city? Bošković puzzled. The delegate gladly answered several of Bošković's questions about Jassy. The city had been mentioned at the beginning of the fifteenth century in one of the charters of Moldovan voivoda Alexandru Buna, said the delegate, but Bošković interrupted him with a question: did you say "voivoda"? Yes, the delegate responded, voivoda—that is the title for Moldovan rulers. It is a Slavic word, said Bošković, and he felt he had met someone familiar at the end of the world. Voivoda Alexandru Lapusneanu named Jassy the capital of Moldova, the delegate continued, while Bošković listened attentively. They have heard of me in this distant duchy, he thought, chiding himself for his arrogance.

Prince Grigory Callimachi received him the following day. He was a young-looking man, with a fashionable moustache with long points, his cheeks clean-shaven, but a long and thick beard. He had round, small eyes, and bushy eyebrows resembling perfect horseshoes. Pater Ruder Bošković, I am so glad you're here, he said. The honor is mine, was Bošković's response. The servants brought out coffee and cakes. The Prince was talkative but dignified. He admired Bošković. He wasn't acting or offering empty flattery, or at least that's how it seemed to Bošković. This is a troubled country, Pater, unfortunate and poor, he spoke. It's a country of bad fortune, but good people. There is a scarcity of light here, but your visit is an indication for me of some future light to come, he said. You wrote about sunspots, he said. My country is a dark spot of this world. A stain on the earth. You wrote about the eclipse of the Sun. The entire history of my country is one great eclipse, that is what he said. Bošković spoke of the beauty of the Moldovan landscape, of rapturous green pastures, of the dazzling view of Jassy. Your hospitality, wisdom, and generosity of mind, Your Highness, are an honor to your country, said Bošković. You spoke beautifully of the Sun and I would like to show you something, perhaps as a gesture of gratitude, he added. I have with me a small instrument that I made in London, he said, an optical device with a small mirror. With its help I can project the picture of the Sun with its clearly visible spots. The Prince was as excited as a child. For a moment even that noble seriousness, that pose of mild indifference and resigned calm, disappeared. All of which soon returned. Is there an instrument, Prince Grigori Callimachi said, will there ever be one, that could show my country readily to people in Europe, that stain on the face of the world, the same way your instrument shows spots on the Sun? This was clearly a sign of parting. Bošković spent three more days in Jassy but did not see the Prince again.

On the night of their departure Bošković told Porter of the impressions that the Prince had left him with. Porter was much less touched by the Prince's hospitality. I suppose it was vanity speaking, Bošković thought. The Prince had clearly shown that he respected me more than Porter. The Prince had not even

received Porter. He said to Bošković: there are many ambassadors but only one Ruđer Bošković. Porter claimed that people
like the Prince were worse than the Ottomans. They have to
show their humility toward Ottomans, he noted, but they are
worse despots to their own citizens than the Ottomans have ever
been. If Moldova is truly a stain on the face of Earth, then it is
not simply a stain but a bruise from Callimachi's whip, Porter
said. If the history of Moldova is really an eclipse of the Sun,
then Callimachi is the Moon's shadow, he added. Yes, that is
what he is, exclaimed Porter at the end, he is simply a shadow of
the Ottoman moon. You are too harsh, Bošković protested, we
are, after all, his guests. He wanted to say more, he wanted to
defend the Prince more passionately, but he made himself stop.
He was, after all, Porter's guest.

They left Jassy on the third of July at early dawn. The carriage
was sliding through the wooden streets as through water. The
Moldovan capital remained behind them, that dark stain on the
face of Earth, as the Prince would have said. They had barely
left Jassy and it already seemed to Bošković that the wooden
city he had just visited did not exist. Porter was planning the
rest of the trip out loud, counting the days and weeks until their
return home. Bošković had a book in his lap, but he didn't care
to open it. The emperors who died two thousand years ago seem
more real to me than the Prince to whom I spoke four days ago,
Bošković thought, feeling guilty in a strange way. The stone
Roman ruins seemed more real than the cultivated wooden city
where he had spent the last five nights. History is more real to
me, he thought, than my own experience. Suetonius seemed
more real to him than his own self.

IV

Poland is near. We've been traveling for forty days. I decided,
already in Istanbul, to write a journal about this trip. Very few

people have the opportunity to travel from the Bosporus to Neva, from the city of Constantine to the city of Peter. The first city has been there for thirteen hundred years, the second hardly fifty. The former was envisioned as a second Rome, the latter as a third Rome. I wasn't born in Rome but I have lived there since I was fourteen and that makes me partially Roman. So a Roman is traveling from the second Rome to the third—that is worth writing about, I thought. I write something every day, in short, mostly facts—numbers and names. Today, it is time to recapitulate.

The second day after we left Istanbul I saw an unforgettable scene. The Tatars, resembling the American redskins from my readings, with their bows and arrows, galloped beside us on wild horses. On that same day, before dusk, we passed a caravan of camels, which was headed toward Istanbul. During the first week of our journey we rested in villages with a predominately Greek population. Their houses were, unfortunately, very dirty. The villagers, though, didn't consider dirt a bad thing. The dirt, as it seems, was the result not of poverty, but of indifference and neglect. It was hard to speak with the Greeks; my vocabulary from classical literature was not very helpful.

On the eighth day of our trip we arrived in the first Bulgarian village. Its name was Kanara. The houses there were modest but clean. This village was much nicer than all the Greek villages we had passed through. I had no difficulty communicating with the villagers. Their language was similar to the language in Dubrovnik. I was pleased with this and immediately asked to speak with the village priest. They brought me a young, twenty-five-year-old man. Bulgarians were Orthodox, and this young man was living proof of a servant of God unrestrained by celibacy: he was married and already had three children. I wondered how a man with his own children could be dedicated to God and his church. Soon though it became clear that the dedication here had serious obstacles. The young man was born in Kanara. He had never left his village, except for one short trip to Istanbul, where he was ordained. I wondered what type of school he could possibly have completed in this small village, realizing soon enough that his ignorance was infinite. This priest's ignorance and the ignorance of his villagers was absolutely incredible. Their understanding of religion comes down to marking Christmas, Easter, the cult of the local Saint, and the worship of the village's miraculous icon. They hardly knew how to cross themselves and they knew no prayers. The most zealous part of their faith was manifested in the fact that, despite everything, they considered themselves Christians, and they would kill anyone who would try to tell them that they hardly had the right to see themselves as such. Despite the common language, I felt a horrible yawning abyss between us. It turns out that it was precisely our common language that separated us. That feeling was, as it seemed, mutual.

The journey through Bulgaria was very emotional. I often thought about my childhood. Because of the language and my age. I am getting older. Sometimes when I wake I don't even know where I am. I find the Slavic world under the Ottomans close to me, close and distant at the same time. I grew up in its shadow, and only now, in my old age, am I actually able to see it. My father was very tied to this part of the world. As I grow older I find myself thinking more and more of him. Time passes, fathers go, sons come. We are still distant and close. I thought about this a great deal, mostly in Novi Pazar. My father often spoke of Novi Pazar. I know it wasn't the same city—the one where my father lived was much closer to Dubrovnik—but those words, the melody in the pronunciation of the name of the place, were the same as my father's. I thought about God's mysterious ways, which brought me at some point in my life, even for a short time, to Novi Pazar. There is a meandering river that passes through Novi Pazar. It is called Kriva, the Crooked River! I know very well how hard it is to establish the etymological origin of most rivers. Yet this is so simple here. In the stories of my childhood rivers could speak. This river truly speaks. In my own language. Afterward I remembered how my father used to say that a job impossible to be done is like straightening a crooked river. Ignorance was everywhere, lack of interest, and a strange complacency.

We traveled through Bulgaria for seven more days: from Novi Pazar to the Danube. I read Suetonius, I thought about Ovid. We were destined to fear the plague in Bulgaria. As always, things end in unpleasantness, precaution, anxiety. I could not just ignore it. When we were in Baltchik, the Bulgarians told us that the plague had appeared in the Turkish quarter. We don't have the plague, they rushed to boast of themselves. There was in this, or I imagined it, more malice against their neighbor than concern for their own skin. The plague doesn't choose Christian or Muslim. The plague sweeps through like death, I thought. My fellow travelers weren't, after all, much different than those narrow-minded Bulgarians. In their foolishness I recognized the strange confidence that the plague can't touch them.

I have seen many rivers in my life, but no river is as mighty as the Danube. The Danube here, near the estuary, near the Black Sea, is black and large like death, dark like Heraclites. A river lying between two worlds, that is how the Danube appears here. We crossed the river, we had suddenly crossed into a different world, as one crosses from childhood into youth. It was the same as when I crossed the Adriatic about forty years ago. Neither then nor now was there the Slavic speech of my childhood on the other bank. At first, to tell the truth, there was nothing. Silence everywhere, untouched land, wilderness. It was beautiful. One finds beauty in the absence of people, I read that somewhere recently.

The land through the looking glass, this is how I always thought about Moldova. I always have optical instruments on my mind, I think about mirrors a great deal, maybe that is why this very thing crossed my mind. On the other hand, I didn't think in this manner about Bulgaria. It's simply as if something mystical were floating over Moldova. The people were different, it wasn't just the language. If I say that Bulgaria is underdeveloped or primitive, it is clearly like this within the world that I find familiar. It is similar enough to other countries that I could compare it to them, even to Bulgaria's detriment. Moldova is difficult to compare with anything, that's how different it is.

On our way to Jassy, the Moldovan capital, we spent a night in a monastery. The monastery felt like a stone from our world, like a countryman I had stumbled upon while abroad. In Bulgaria, I'd consider this sort of monastery a symbol of difference. Here, such a monastery evoked something familiar. I was reminded there, in that monastery, of the Portuguese king who had invited me to Brasilia on a mission to make the first map of his large colony. I had the most polite excuse to decline his kind invitation—that same year the Holy Father entrusted me with a job that required I stay in Rome. I remember, though, how relieved I felt that I was able to refuse the king in such a simple way. I feared the distant and the unknown. I feared neither the distant nor the unknown. I feared the unknown distant. Moldova is strange, Moldova is unknown, but it is close. It's close to Europe. Moldova is a country within Europe's reach.

The capital city always represents the best and the worst of a given country. Paris is elegant and arrogant, London majestic and righteous. I am curious about Petrograd. I was curious about Jassy. I imagined Jassy would be the most beautiful and unusual city, as if from a storybook, a dream. And indeed, that's how it was.

Moldova resembled, as I said, the land through the looking glass. A city of wood appeared from a distance as a theater stage. Once I approached the city, however, I realized that my comparison didn't do justice to the place. Jassy was too luxuriant, too real, and too alive. My Dubrovnik is more stage-like, I thought.

We were the Prince's guests. I walked toward his residence as if I were approaching a castle from a fairy tale. The Moldovan seal, carved everywhere in wood, was very special. In the middle of it there was a bull's head, above it a six-pointed star, and underneath, a sun and half-moon.

The Prince's delegate was the type of man in whom European refinement and Moldovan exoticism were combined. I asked him about the origin of the name of the country. The country Moldova was named for its river, Moldova. How did the river get its name, I asked, having a presentiment that the answer wouldn't be as simple as was the case in Novi Pazar. What else is one to expect in a fairy-tale country but a fairy tale? And what he told me was indeed a fairy tale. Once upon a time a Voivoda had started . . . but I immediately cut him off: a Voivoda? He confirmed, a Voivoda, that *is how Moldovans call their princes, and my heart livened up at the sound of that Slavic word. This Voivoda, together with his dog, went hunting for a monster. The monster was keeping a young beauty captive. The Voivoda, as it happens in such tales, freed the beautiful girl and slayed the monster. His dog helped him in the fight, but was killed. The dog's name was Molda. The Voivoda named the river after his dog. The Voivoda and the beautiful girl lived together, I added. The delegate was confused: I actually don't know, the tale mentions nothing like that, it ends with the naming of the river.*

The delegate announced that the Prince, our host, wished to receive me the following day: Your reputation has reached this small, distant country. He relayed the Prince's message to me, out of courtesy, I thought. The next day, however, I realized that these words were spoken in all sincerity.

A prince worthy of his country is Georgi Callimachi. He received me wholeheartedly, as a friend, with coffee and cake. He was eloquent, learned, and wise. Yet again it seemed at times that he had gained his knowledge in some magical way, not by studying or reading. He really knew a great deal about me and my work. He spoke of his country with melancholy, in the manner of some unfortunate Shakespearian king, that is how he appeared to me, like a tame river: all the power, nowhere to spill over. He did not hide his quiet joy at our encounter; I trusted the joy, but I also trusted that he was relieved when our conversation was over.

I hoped to see the Prince again, at least once more during the three remaining days, but did not. I was a bit disappointed. The Prince, however, did not even once receive Ambassador Porter, my fellow traveler. The Ambassador hardly managed to conceal his anger over this. The mighty English crown stood behind him, yet some local nobleman had snubbed him. The Ambassador is not used to such a thing, despite having spent all these years in the Orient. To make matters worse, the Prince received me, a man behind whom nothing stood but his own work. Porter's moral tirades were meant to sound principled, but it was clear that they were set off by his hurt feelings. So many negative traits Porter tried to attribute to

*our host. He did not, however, ruin my impressions. I don't find
Callimachi to be a saint, but he seems to me nobler than all the
European aristocrats I have met in my life. In a more fortunate
country this nobility would have been more visible. In the Prince's
courage to contemptuously position himself against the representative
of the English crown, Porter recognized, or pretended to recognize,
only the obverse of humility before the Ottomans. Such reasoning
revealed Porter's defense before his own humiliation.*

*When we left Jassy at dawn I thought about Prince Callimachi.
He remains in his small, unfortunate, and most beautiful city.
The capital and this entire country will soon become a dream-like
memory. We passed through Bulgaria. What mostly lingers in my
memory of that place are images of ignorance and backwardness.
From Moldova I carry images of beauty, wasteland, fear, and
dream. I'm on my way to Petrograd, yet it feels as if I'm actually
going to Moldova, to Jassy. It's as if this country has charmed me,
but I mustn't forget: I'm going to Petrograd, to the Third Rome,
Moldova is just a country on my way from the Second to the Third
Rome. There will never be a Rome in Moldova. I'm in Moldova
now and I will never be back. Moldova is a country I am about to
leave forever. Farewell Moldova. Poland is near.*

V

You have been writing for a while, Pater, remarked Porter. I don't
take the *Nulla dies sine linea* literally, so I make up for it occasionally. He paused for a moment and then continued. Even if a
day passes without writing a line, the day comes to draw the line.
What do you mean? asked Porter. You draw the line through
everything at some point, replied Bošković, I'm slowly beginning
to draw the line through this journey, our journey together. Yes,
responded Porter thoughtfully, we are going to the West, you
further eastward. We met on the Bosporus, we'll part ways on
the Dniester, he continued. There is a new world north of the
Dniester, thought Bošković. The fourth world. The first is my

world, our world. The second is the Ottoman world—Istanbul and Bulgaria. The third is some inter-world, limbo, Moldova. Above them is the fourth world—Russia. This is already at the gates of Russia. Zaleszczyki was ahead of them, the city of old Count Poniatowski.

At last, an encounter with a true European nobleman, Porter rejoiced. He is still wounded from Jassy, Bošković thought, though he was curious as well. Stanislaw Poniatowski had been celebrated in Western Europe by Voltaire. The Count was more than ninety years old—almost a hundred, but he was still very strong. His city was the last stop this unusual caravan would make. The company was already getting ready to return to Istanbul. Porter would stay here with his family for another day or two, Bošković somewhat longer: both in Zaleszczyki and in nearby Kamieniec—there was a Jesuit school here which he intended to visit.

Bošković remembered that Poniatowski envisioned Zaleszczyki as a small Petrograd. The city was, as it appeared at first sight, deliberate. As if the Dniester were embracing the city. The city resembled an island in a broken ring of the river. True, the city was not raised on unbroken ground, this was an old settlement, but in the past few years the city had been expanded and renovated. For Poniatowski, the city was a symbol, a model, and a window. All of this could be seen at the Count's palace, even though it wasn't finished. The palace had been under construction for years. Every time, just before the construction workers were about to place the last stone, the Count would make new plans for further expansion. The work on the outer reaches of the palace astonished Bošković. But when he came to the central part he realized that the palace wasn't actually any less beautiful than the Roman palaces he had visited. As he walked toward his chambers he was constructing the sentence he would write down in his journal. The space is set out optimally as in the most civilized parts of Europe. That is why one breathes here more easily and freely, after such a long and interminable space of total barbarism.

Bošković went to sleep briefly in his chambers. He wanted to be rested for the evening. He was to dine with Count Poniatowski and other local nobility.

The old Count appeared both strong and very fragile. He was a big man, thin, with very strong bones. His face was clean-shaven. He had a high forehead and a very pronounced jaw. He spoke Italian fluently yet somewhat archaically. With some strange pride he mentioned that the family Poniatowski originated from the Florentine family Torelli. The origin meant more to him than his own achievements, at least so it seemed. Bošković remarked on the grandeur of the palace, and the Count responded: the more I build the more I cheat death. The noblemen present protested the old man's words: you'll live for a long time, they chirped together. The Count dismissed them with a wave. Somewhat scornfully Bošković surveyed the company gathered at the table. These noblemen were scented, well dressed, but more than anything they were quite comical. Comical was their attempt to resemble the French as much as they could. They copied Western fashion: from clothing to the topics of conversation. Even the dinner looked like French dinners, although the preparation was much worse. Bošković ate slowly and quietly. Porter chatted with Poniatowski. Beatrice didn't even try to hide her sneer and boredom. One young fellow even attempted to include her in the conversation. She just treated him rudely and haughtily, worse than her own servants.

On the morning of the following day the Porters continued their trip to Kraków, and further toward England. The Ambassador parted ways with Bošković affectionately, while Beatrice remained entirely indifferent. Little Anne Margaret kissed him on the cheek.

Around noon Bošković went for a walk. He planned to stay in Zaleszczyki for two more days. One of the Count's guests from last night, who was to leave for Kamieniec in two days, invited Bošković to travel with him.

His leg had almost stopped hurting. It was as if the previous night's encounter with Poniatowski had made him younger. He is twice my age, Bošković thought while strolling the streets of Zaleszczyki. The city is pretty, yet somehow—Bošković was looking for the right word—ordinary. He knew, however, why he had that impression. Every future city, he feared, from now on would seem ordinary, as is the case with any city when compared to Jassy, the wooden city from a fairy tale. Bošković walked fast, he whipped the facades with his eyes, looking back to Jassy. He came to the city square, where he noticed an unusual house, a wooden house, or at least it seemed wooden to him. He started moving resolutely toward it, one step, two, three, four, five, six, and then, stumble, water, pain, darkness.

He regained consciousness in bed. He was in his chambers again, in the Count's palace. He was almost entirely naked and still a bit bloody. He was cold and his leg ached terribly.

You fell into a well, a man said to him. His head went hazy again. He was shaky, but he knew he was being helped with dressing, that he was being carried to the carriage, a great carriage with six horses. They laid him down in the carriage. The horses moved.

He was getting dizzy. He was fading. The carriage was shaking. They were stopping again. They were taking him out. His brothers, the Jesuits, were there. This was Kamieniec. This was the school. This was where they were taking him. The bed, again. The dream, again. The pain.

The fever. The pain. Time was passing. One morning he woke clearheaded. How long have I been here? he asked one of the younger Jesuits. Six days.

He received visitors regularly. He knew six of the Jesuits in the Kamieniec school from Rome. They hadn't been in Rome for a long time, longer than he. They asked about the news, about mutual acquaintances.

He was feeling better. The shock had passed, so had the fever, but his leg ached more than ever. He had trouble walking. Without the cane he could barely take two or three steps. They took good care of him but he wasn't used to being a burden to anyone. He almost lost his sense of time: he did not know the date or the day of the week. He wasn't reading or writing. He gave up his journey to Petrograd. Or rather, he accepted the fact that he couldn't go. With a leg like that he couldn't even think about such a long trip. Giving up the trip didn't seem to bother him. He wanted to see Petrograd, he had been looking forward to it, and now it almost didn't matter to him. He knew, knew very well, that he would never reach Petrograd, that he wouldn't see it in his lifetime. The Count's hundred years did not provide him consolation. His own fifty were too much.

In Warsaw they have better physicians, his Jesuit brothers told him. They organized a trip to Warsaw. There, he was hosted by the old Count's sons: Mikhail and Stanislav, the future Polish king. Bošković was a guest in the Count's Warsaw residence. At the end of summer the Count planned to come to Warsaw to visit Bošković. The Count's son told Bošković of the Count's remorse over the Jesuit's regrettable fall in Zaleszczyki. At the end of August, however, the news arrived: Count Poniatowski had died. Deep old age, yet an unexpected death, thought Bošković.

He met many doctors but each one of them had a different opinion about his leg. His condition was gradually improving, mostly on its own. As in Istanbul, Bošković spent most of his time with ambassadors. The Austrian, Mercy, the Russian, Kayserling, and the Frenchman, de Baulmy, replaced Porter.

Autumn passed rather quickly. After that the long northern winter arrived. Bošković went out very rarely. The cold air did not agree with him. He feared the snow and the ice, he was afraid of slipping, he was repelled by the somber horizon of the short days.

He tried to organize his days well. He slept as much as he could. He ate often and very slowly. He read every day for at least three hours. He organized the notes from his journey. His thoughts often wandered off to the times of his travels with Porter, which is why he actually returned to them. The entries in the journal served as a proof that all of this had indeed happened. The days after the fall, the days after the misfortune and delirium, the days of feverous trance almost painted the other days in his memory with the colors of illusion and fantasy. Karnobat exists, Jenibazar exists, Jassy exists, Bošković repeated to himself in a whisper. It all exists. The summer exists, Dubrovnik exists, life exists, so he spoke.

The winter was severe, severe and awfully long, almost unbearable. Spring arrived and with it an opportunity to travel South—home. Prince Liechtenstein was traveling to Pisa so he invited Bošković to travel with him in his carriage. They left in the month of May. Bošković had another summer journey ahead of him. In the early autumn he returned to the Mediterranean, before the winter he was in Rome.

Bošković lived for another quarter of a century, but he didn't leave familiar territory. Soon after his journey to the East he settled in Milan. He taught at the University of Pavia, and observed the sky from the Milan observatory. In the year 1767 the Royal Society of London invited Bošković to join their expedition to America in order to observe the next transit of Venus over the Sun. Despite his chronically painful leg Bošković very much wanted to go. California, he said to himself, California, another country with a magical name. Bošković's strong wish was not, however, granted. The Jesuits weren't in the Pope's favor. High politics stood in the way of astronomy.

Bošković looked for a cure for his lame leg everywhere. He even went to Paris to Doctor Morando, but all in vain. He returned to Milan disappointed. He dreamt about another trip to Poland, about returning to Dubrovnik, but found a new home in Paris. In 1773 the Pope abolished the Jesuit order. Bošković was desperate: he lost his title and identity, he felt almost "like an orphan." He needed a new patron. He would find one in Paris, at the House of Bourbon, primarily in Louis the XV and, after his death, in Louis XVI.

In Paris Bošković began to sum up his life. He worked on a great long poem about the eclipse and oversaw its translation into

French. In 1779 he dedicated the poem to French King Louis the XVI. Such were the rules of this world, thought Bošković. Even though the poem about the eclipse belonged more to the Prince of the land of the eclipse, certainly more than to the king who reigned in the city of lights, to the descendant of a king who had named himself the Sun. There was something dire in this dedication, or so it seemed to Bošković.

After his seventieth birthday Bošković returned to Milan. His leg ached again and he felt quite weak, but he was calm. He had lived out the years given to man by God. He often thought about his journey from Istanbul to Poland. He had trouble concentrating, he wrote rarely, hardly ever read. At night he liked to observe the sky. He was more and more convinced that some form of life existed out there, among the stars.

He oversaw the publication of his collected works. As more volumes saw the light of day, his own mind darkened. He talked to himself. He spoke of the East, of its ignorance, filth, barbarism, misfortune, and beauty.

In September 1786 his friends took him to the former Jesuit school in Monza. There Antonio Daneti arranged for his accommodation and care. Bošković's condition worsened. He was sad, awfully sad. I wasted my life, Bošković used to say. It is my fault, it is all my fault. His friends consoled him, but in vain. He even thought of suicide. A fog had covered his thoughts. Through the fog he envisioned the contours of the Bulgarian, Moldovan, and Polish landscapes. The images popped up: the waves of the Danube, the fields of tulips, the city of wood. There were no letters, no figures, there were none of these in his thoughts now, only the world, only life. He was much weaker, much more distant from the people who took care of him. On Christmas he thought about Anne Margaret Porter, about the child who was no longer a child. Not much longer, he said to Luigi Tomagnini on New Year's Eve. The days were getting longer but the darkness and the fog in Bošković's consciousness seldom cleared. Even when he spoke to himself, his speech was garbled for all who heard him, and probably to himself as well. On the eleventh of February he started to cough blood. He died on Tuesday, on the thirteenth of February, at eleven a.m.

Comet

The Orient is the greatest wonder and biggest horror. The border between life and death is not clearly delineated there, but meanders and wavers.

Ivo Andrić: *Signs by the Roadside*

1

THE FIRST GIFT SHE REMEMBERS getting was a mirror. For her fourth birthday her father gave her a small, oval mirror, an ordinary mirror in a green frame. She couldn't imagine a better gift.

Daddy's little princess, he used to call her. A mirror for Daddy's princess, a mirror that does not lie, a mirror for the most beautiful girl, a magical mirror, he said. If you wish to know who is the most beautiful girl in the whole world, just ask your mirror, take a look at it and you will get your answer, he said to her, and she laughed happily.

She loved Snow White. This was her favorite fairy tale. She had fallen in love with mirrors even before Snow White. You used to cry a lot when you were a baby, her dad used to say to her, you were a crybaby, you cried all the time. We used to give you toys, he said, dolls, little bears, and rattles, but nothing helped. It was only when you got hold of your mom's mirror that the crying stopped. One morning, while you were still asleep, your mom wanted to put her makeup on. She retrieved the mirror, he said, and you burst into tears. From then on you always slept with the mirror, he told her. Other girls sleep with plush toys, my girl with a mirror. Do you know why? he asked for the hundredth time. She had heard this story many times, she had heard this question many times, and the answer, which she knew, but she shook her head. It is the greatest thing in the world to hear your dad saying: it is because my girl is the most beautiful girl in the world.

You will spoil her, said grandma. She always said that whenever Dad said to his little girl that she was the most beautiful in the world. Grandma is Dad's mom, Maria Alexandra knew. Grandma was mad because he loved his daughter more than his own mother. Maria Alexandra was not sure why her grand-mother would get mad. She too loved her dad more than her mom.

Grandma was the only person who called her Alexandra. That was strange because Grandma's name was also Alexandra. Grandma wanted Dad to name her Alexandra, such was the tradition in the family, as Grandma said. It is not as if Dad didn't obey. She was named Alexandra, and not simply Alexandra, but Maria Alexandra, it was only that everyone called her Maria, except Grandma who called her Alexandra.

She really liked her name. Maria Alexandra, it was so long, so charming, so unusual. Not one girl in daycare had such a pretty name. No girl was as pretty as she was. She was named Alexandra after Grandma. She was named Maria after the most beautiful woman in the world.

She was named after Maria Cebotari, the singer and actress, the most beautiful Moldovan woman, the woman with whom Grandpa—Dad's dad—was in love before he married Grandma. Maria Alexandra knew her grandpa only from the photographs. Grandpa died three months before she was born. Had Maria Alexandra been born as a boy she would have been named after her grandpa. This way she has two names, one for each of Grandpa's loves.

On the thirteenth of February 1990, on her fourth birthday, Maria Alexandra received a gift from her father—a little mirror from which she never parted. No gift ever meant to her as much as this mirror. Every thirteenth of February she received gifts. Every thirteenth of February Grandma remarked that he'd spoil her. Every thirteenth of February Maria Alexandra grew more and more beautiful. Every thirteenth of February Maria Alexandra loved her father more.

Her father was a high-school geography teacher. The whole of Cahul called him Gagarin. Her father conducted an astronomy section. He spoke about the stars with enthusiasm. In places like Cahul people laugh at enthusiasm. Her dad loved the stars. He loved her and the stars.

Mother worked in the court. She traveled often. She used to stay at work for a long time. She worked in the summer and in winter. During school holidays Dad was always with Maria Alexandra. They played, laughed, talked. As Maria Alexandra grew up their conversations became more serious.

He told her about life during the Soviet Union. He explained the circumstances around its breakdown and how Moldova became independent. He talked about the history of their region, about battles and wars surrounding Cahul, about the Russians and the Ottomans. He told her stories from the family history. She found out that Maria Cebotari's was truly Grandpa's first love and that Grandma still hated Maria Cebotari even though she had died before Dad was born. She learned that Grandpa wanted to name his daughter Maria, but he only had a son, Dad. So Dad, in honor of his father, named his daughter Maria.

He told her about the sky, about stars, about comets. He told her that she was born in the year of the passing of Halley's Comet, just like Maria Cebotari—she was born in 1910 when Halley's Comet was passing by the Earth. You were born seventy-six years later, during the next passing of the comet, he told her. The story about Halley's Comet is the story of the human race, he said. The Chinese noticed it thousands of years ago. Babylonians wrote about the passing of the comet. The star of Bethlehem was in fact Halley's Comet. The comet passed by Earth during the Battle of Hastings, and when the Ottomans besieged Belgrade. Kepler wrote about it, but Halley was the first to recognize it so it was named after him. The comet was photographed for the first time in the year that Maria Cebotari was born. The most people anticipated its appearance during the year you were born, her dad told her. As long as there is humankind people will be looking at the sky and every three-quarters of a century they will be looking for Halley's Comet.

He told her about foreign lands and cities, about places he had wanted to visit when he was young. He told her about New York, Istanbul, Dubrovnik. On the thirteenth of February he gave her a postcard of Dubrovnik. He talked about the war in

Yugoslavia, about the destruction of Dubrovnik, he told her about the fear of war.

In the fall of 1993 Maria Alexandra started school. She didn't like school but she liked to talk to her dad about it. She couldn't wait to go to high school, to go every day to the school where her dad worked. Dad is much smarter than a teacher, she thought, Dad is the smartest in the world.

Sometimes, late in the evening, when she lay awake in bed, Maria Alexandra eavesdropped on her mom and dad's conversation in the adjacent room. How different Dad was with her! With Maria he was always cheerful, he laughed and joked. When he talked to her mom his face darkened, became worrisome and serious. They discussed politics, their situation, finances. Maria Alexandra sometimes didn't know which was the real Dad: the one who grumbled and swore, or the one who played with her and talked about stars.

As Maria Alexandra was growing up, Dad began discussing the things with her that he discussed with Mom, though always in a more cheerful tone and with more optimism. In 1997 she had a geography class and she enjoyed asking Dad about things that weren't—particularly—clear to her. Dad's responses were long and long-winded. He'd finally start telling things to himself rather than to her. He told her about the eternal misfortunes of the East, about the damnation of their homeland and its backwater beauty, about rivers, old cities, about glorious history.

On the thirteenth of February 1998, Mom and Dad bought her pants she had wanted for a long time, pants from the most expensive boutique shop in Cahul. Grandma spoke again about spoiling her, she looked at her sullenly, but now in a new way. A few days after her birthday Mom explained that she was about to become a woman, but she already knew that.

At school Maria Alexandra kept to herself. She stood out only by her quiet beauty. She wasn't a teachers' pet, but she had good grades. She didn't have a best friend, or a permanent circle to which she belonged, but she was not an outcast. She was different.

That day it rained terribly. She came home, soaked to the skin. Dad sat in the dark. What happened? she asked. Mom had an accident, he said. She was on her way to perform a coroner's inquest, he said. They crashed into a truck, he said. She is dead, he said.

The funeral. Grandma spent fifteen days with them. She wanted to stay longer, but Dad wouldn't let her. Maria Alexandra was happy about that. She is already fifteen, she is in high school, she can take care of herself and Dad.

On the thirteenth of February 2002 her dad bought her Maria Cebotari's CD with the arias of Mozart, Strauss, Bizet, and Verdi, which they enjoyed that evening. Her dad often shut his eyes while the voice of the woman after whom she was named reverberated in the room. Maria Alexandra was a little bored, but she'd never admit it to her dad. More than listening to music she liked to listen to her dad talk. Dad talked about François de Tott, eighteenth-century baron, who was in Moldova almost two hundred and fifty years ago, and who met a Turk in Moldova—Ali-Aga. The Turk from his memoirs was so much like Mozart's Osman, as if he had crossed over to Mozart's *The Abduction from the Seraglio*. Moldova was indebted to Mozart, and Maria Cebotari repaid the debt, Dad said. He spoke about Hauterive, about Gibbon, Rousseau, Voltaire. They all wrote about Moldova, he said. Today we are the most wretched place in Europe, he said. They know us for our misfortune or they don't know us at all. On a TV show a rich woman was marrying a Moldovan prince, as if Moldova were some non-existent country from a fairy tale. On the wedding day the terrorists kill them all, Dad told her. He drank vodka that evening and chain-smoked.

The evenings of drinking became more common. Dad was never a bad drunk: it's only that he talked faster, became tongue-tied, and went to bed earlier. Soon she realized that he drank in secret, but she didn't say anything about it, so everything went back to normal.

Maria Alexandra rarely went out except to go shopping and to school. Go out, her dad used to say to her, don't shut yourself in. She nodded and continued doing her thing. She didn't like going out: sitting on broken benches in dark parks, screaming out in noisy local cafés with beaming neon lights. Sometimes she took a walk in one of Cahul's tree-lined streets, and that was enough for her. She liked to cook for herself and her dad, she liked watching films on the VCR, she liked to listen to her dad's stories about childhood, about the army, about his studies, how he met her mom, about her birth, how she fell in love with mirrors. She liked looking at herself in the mirror. She didn't use makeup, but she liked to observe her reflection in the mirror: the outline of her lips, the eyelashes, the perfect arc of her eyebrows, the glimmer of her teeth, the blueness of her eyes.

One boy, a senior, sometimes drew her attention. She used to see him in the hallways of the school. He was shy. He always looked at her in passing, but that was all. Soon, however, he went to the university. She saw him one summer's eve: they passed each other while walking along a tree-lined street. He embraced a girl Maria didn't know, but he looked at her this time as well.

On the thirteenth of February 2003 her father gave her a book by Czesław Miłosz, *Native Realm*. That evening he didn't drink. He asked her whether she was thinking about her future, what she wanted to study, what she would like to do. It's still very early to think about all these things, she said, but her dad didn't give up. My main concern is to be here, with you, she finally said. Her dad got angry at that point, for the first time. That matters least of all, he said, don't waste your life. Go away as far as you can, he said, to Paris—that would be best—and stay there. Get out of here, he said, from this darkness. This isn't life, he said, this is life in eclipse. I want you to be happy, she said on the verge of tears. I would be the happiest if you left, he said.

In the morning, however, they behaved as if they had forgotten last night. A few days later her dad tried to continue the conversation. You are right, he said, maybe it is too early to think about this, but please start thinking about your future. You are young, smart, the most beautiful in the world. Your life is ahead of you, make something of it. You can come to visit Cahul several times a year. I will live for those days and I will be happy every time I think about you. I will, I will think about it, Maria Alexandra said, even though she knew she didn't want to go anywhere.

On the eighth of June, at the end of the school year, someone burst into Maria Alexandra's classroom during biology class. The teacher, said the flustered student, the teacher fell, it's the geography teacher. Maria Alexandra ran out and into the neighboring room. Her father lay dead under the map of Europe.

2

When she started school in September it felt like she had slept through the entire summer. Twelfth grade, the last, graduation, a new school, a new class, a new city, Chisinau.

Her grandma had arrived the same night three months ago, on the eighth of June. In Maria Alexandra's memory, the image of Grandma's face immediately overlay the image of her father's still body on the classroom floor. She did not remember the hours in between.

That's how all those three months seemed to her: two or three dozen loosely connected scenes. The hole in her memory was significantly smaller than the hole in her heart.

Grandma organized the funeral, Grandma picked up her report card, and she arranged for a temporary guardianship—until the thirteenth of February of the next year and Maria Alexandra's eighteenth birthday. Grandma withdrew Maria Alexandra from the school in Cahul and enrolled her in a school in Chisinau. Grandma rented out their apartment in Cahul to a young couple and brought Maria Alexandra to her place in Chisinau. Maria Alexandra simply surrendered herself to her new situation. In September, when classes started, it crossed her mind that she could have asked Grandma to stay in Cahul so that she could finish school there, but it was too late now. Even if I'd asked her, she thought, it would have been the same.

The school was pretty far away from Grandma's house. She had to walk much more than she did in Cahul. The students from her neighborhood mostly traveled by bus. Grandma told Maria Alexandra right at the beginning that traveling by city bus is a pure waste of money. Is it so bad to take a nice walk for twenty minutes, she asked rhetorically, in the blossom of your youth?

The walks from school and back were the best part of her day. The early autumn was very beautiful, gentle golden autumn. She enjoyed passing through parks and alleys, stepping on the leaves, she enjoyed the moments when the chestnuts fell on her. She enjoyed looking at multicolored tree branches as if they were fireworks; she enjoyed the smell of ozone. She enjoyed light rain and the wind. When she arrived in the schoolyard all enjoyment stopped.

From the outside the school looked more like a prison than a school, big gray building with square windows. It appeared cold and threatening. It was actually inside of the building where the real unpleasantness began. Low ceilings, flashing lights in the hallways, brown ceramic tiles on the walls.

She was treated as an intruder by her new class. She was too beautiful and did not fit in: the girls hated her, the boys feared her. They all ignored her, there were sneers, gossip. Poor girl, they said, provincial, so odd.

The teachers were uninterested. It was all much more alienating than in Cahul. But that didn't bother Maria Alexandra. She enjoyed the isolation, she enjoyed the solitude.

Her joyful walks were interrupted by her grandma's house. The torture began at the front door. Where have you been? Where did you stop by? Grandma asked, even though she walked faster home than to school. Go eat and study, she said as soon as Maria Alexandra shed her shoes. There were ordinarily some thin soups or stews at the table. Maria Alexandra always ate very little. Now she had to put up with her grandma's nagging. The lady doesn't like the supper, they spoiled you, is the little Miss on a diet, Grandma would say.

After supper she went to a room Grandma referred to as the maid's room. You must study, repeated Grandma. Maria Alexandra liked those two or three hours at dusk. She sat at a table, opened her textbook, and pretended to read. In fact she was thinking about the past, she was remembering.

She tried to remember everything, to carve into her memory details about her dad, her mom, her childhood. She tried to recall all her birthdays, the conversations, the moments. She wished to count her memories, classify them, and preserve them. If she didn't do that, she thought, they would all combine, blur, merge into a single amalgam, and the only image she remembered would be her father's body on the classroom floor.

She entered her grandma's room as soon as it was dark. There was one light bulb burning there. Grandma tried to save electricity, so in the evenings they were always together in one room. They turned the TV on only for the news.

Golden autumn passed quickly. The cold days were coming. The walks to school and back were not so pleasant anymore. The time spent at school now had one advantage: it was warm.

Grandma saved on gas. A meager pension, two mouths to feed, she said, it was hard on her own, especially now. Maria Alexandra knew that Grandma received two pensions, her father's pension, a pension that belonged to her. Grandma always said she was saving that money for Maria Alexandra's studies— money for university tuition. This is your education fund, she said, I will not spend a penny on other things.

The afternoons and evenings were now cold. Maria Alexandra had to wear a shirt and thick sweater while she pretended to study. As the days grew shorter, they went to bed earlier. Maria Alexandra usually couldn't fall asleep for a long time, but at least she was warm under the blankets. Now she went over her memories in the dark.

It started snowing at the end of November. She was as happy as a child about it. She hadn't felt cheerful in so long. The snow, like a bandage, covered her wounded world. It was the first day she entered the Chisinau school smiling.

It was at that time that she started studying more seriously. The night and bed were left for reminiscing, but the afternoon was for studying. Her dad always looked forward to her good grades, she thought, Dad wanted her to do well in school, to study at a good university.

December passed quickly for Maria Alexandra: Christmas, New Year's, the end of first semester. She was pleased with her grades. They were not all As, but she had a full semester to improve. While she walked the decorated streets of Chisinau, toward Grandma's house, she thought for the first time about her studies. It wasn't what she'd study, but, more importantly, where? Not in Chisinau, she thought, not in Moldova. Dad wanted her to go to Europe, to the world, to the West.

During the holidays she helped Grandma with the household chores. I can do it, Alexandra, Grandma said, I can do it myself, you just sit and study. It was difficult to explain to Grandma that she didn't need to study since she was on holidays. At this point Maria Alexandra would open the book again and daydream. Only now she didn't think about the past but about the future.

In her notebook she had the names and codes for the European countries. She quietly read the names of the countries and continued daydreaming. She sounded out the name of Austria, and remembered the movie *Before Sunrise*, Mozart, and Maria Cebotari. She said France and thought about Paris, Bizet, the Arc de Triomphe. She read Italy with images of the Coliseum passing through her mind, together with the taste of oregano and a powerful torrent of Verdi's arias. At dusk she would close her journal and move to Grandma's room. The night was for memories.

At the beginning of the second semester, Maria Alexandra started searching the Internet for information about studies abroad. In one classroom there were several computers. Maria Alexandra used every school break for research. At first she was excited about the multitude of possibilities. Soon enough she realized that many of these opportunities were just illusions.

The first problem was the language, the second—expenses. The only foreign language Maria Alexandra ever studied was English. Farewell Austria, farewell France, farewell Italy, she thought. Even if she knew all the languages in the world, she said to herself, it would be impossible because of the expense.

After the initial excitement, she was overcome by disappointment. Meanwhile the two extremes found a middle ground. There were universities in Austria, France, and Italy, where classes were taught in English: there were possibilities for stipends, loans, work-study programs. There were many choices but nothing was simple.

She needed to go to the British Consulate to take the English language test. She needed to apply to several universities in order to be accepted, perhaps, to one. There were stipends to apply for. At the same time she needed to study and keep up her good grades in the second semester. Most importantly, she needed to finish high school to have any chance of attending a university. Maria Alexandra decided this was the priority. Afterward, I hope I'll be able to enter a university abroad, in Europe, any one of them.

Then came the thirteenth of February 2004, her birthday, her eighteenth, the first one without her dad, and the grief returned. Her enthusiasm melted with the last snow of that winter. Instead of going to the computer room, she went outside that day on her break. Two girls, they seemed to be freshmen, smoked in the little park. Maria Alexandra approached them and asked for a cigarette. That is how she started smoking.

Grandma gave her some money. Buy yourself something Alexandra, she said, for your birthday. It will be enough for ten packs, Maria Alexandra thought. The next morning on her way to school she bought a pack and a small red lighter.

She could sense the spring. She enjoyed smoking more and more. In the morning, as soon as she was out of sight of Grandma's house, she lit a cigarette. I look older because of the cigarettes, people look at me differently.

A colleague from her class, Helen, approached her once during the break and asked for a lighter. Mine died, she said. She lit a cigarette but didn't move away. I envy your complexion, she said to Maria Alexandra, I'm not so pale even with powder.

Helen was a Goth. Her clothes were always black, her hair dyed black, thick black makeup on her face. She was lonely, a poor student, and often skipped classes. I'm skipping math she said to Maria Alexandra, stubbing out her cigarette. Me too, she responded, I'm coming with you.

They went into a bar. It was not far from school, but Maria Alexandra had never been on that street. It was dark inside, as if it were evening. She followed Helen to a little booth. Passing by the bar Helen waved at a guy sitting at the bar. He had longish hair and a leather jacket. That was Boško, Helen said, he is Yugoslav.

Maria Alexandra looked at the price list. It's lucky I have some of the money left that Grandma gave me, she thought. I have money, Helen said, don't worry, a round of vodka is on me.

Helen paid for the first round, Maria Alexandra for the second. Maria Alexandra often looked at her watch. I have to come home at the same time as if I were coming from school, she explained. They left the bar together. Boško suddenly appeared before them. Helen, won't you introduce me to your friend? he said in English. They shook hands. I am going this way, Helen said. Grandma's house was on the other side of town. I will go the other way, Maria Alexandra said. Me too, Boško said, let's go together.

He was talkative and charming. I am twenty-three, he said, I've been here two or three months, on business. How do you know Helen? she asked. She's always in that bar, Boško said, I frequent the place as well, I live nearby. Helen says you're from Yugoslavia. I am, Boško said, from the former Yugoslavia. It doesn't exist any longer but more people know about Yugoslavia than about Croatia. You're from Croatia? Maria Alexandra exclaimed. Have you ever been to Dubrovnik? I live in Dubrovnik, replied Boško. My dad often spoke about Dubrovnik, Maria Alexandra said. Boško looked in her eyes. He died recently, she added, and lowered her look. I'm sorry, said Boško. They were already near Grandma's house. It was nice meeting you, said Maria Alexandra. It was nice meeting you too, said Boško.

She ate very little that afternoon. If she hadn't been cheerful Grandma would have thought she was sick. The flu comes with spring, she used to say. While she pretended to study, Maria Alexandra thought more about the bar she had visited than about her school and universities. When she lay down Boško's face intruded on her memories. Probably because of Dubrovnik. She slept fitfully. At dawn she found a postcard of Dubrovnik among her things and stared at it for a while. On the way to school she had two cigarettes. She walked fast and arrived at school earlier than usual. She looked at her watch, thought for a second, turned around, and went toward the bar. She entered somewhat tentatively and headed for the booth where she had sat yesterday with Helen. Boško was sitting at the bar. He was having coffee. Maria Alexandra, he exclaimed cheerfully, what are you doing here?

3

Boško knew how to listen. He actually knew how to get her to talk, and then he knew how to listen. There are people who know how to create trust, to simulate desire for confession, but afterward they don't know how to listen. Or they just can't wait to start talking about themselves. Or they remain dully quiet and stare listlessly, nodding. Boško was different. He listened attentively and identified with her. He let her know, with his gestures and short sentences, that he understood and sympathized.

He didn't rush her either. At first they just spoke about school and books. When he realized she was skipping school he almost got upset. You must go to school, he said, I will always be happy to wait for you afterward. After classes we can go for a walk.

This became a small ritual. Boško waited for Maria Alexandra after school and walked her almost to her grandma's door. During those walks Maria Alexandra talked and talked. You're a smart and brave young lady, he told her once. You're peripatetic but not pathetic. You know about peripatetics? he asked her, and she, half-smiling, responded: you know, we too have philosophy in our schools.

Soon their walks became too short for them. They began walking slower, but Maria Alexandra, every now and then, looked at her watch. I have to go straight home after school because of my grandma, she said. It's because of Grandma you walk me just to my door. Grandmas are naïve, Boško once said. If you tell her that you need to stay an hour longer at school to prepare for your graduation exam, I don't think she'd suspect anything.

So it was. Spring started, the days became longer, Maria Alexandra went with Boško after school to the bar where they usually met. There they talked, sometimes had coffee, sometimes vodka, and afterward Boško walked her home. Now you know almost everything about me, Maria Alexandra told him one afternoon before they parted, tomorrow we'll talk about you.

I don't like talking about myself, Boško told her the next morning. I'm quiet, reserved, an introvert, he added, I've been always like that. She was getting ready to say something, but Boško interrupted her: last night I was thinking that I want to tell you things I haven't told others.

He said that his name wasn't Boško but Bogoljub. Boško is a nickname, he said, not many people know my real name; only the customs officials who look at my passport, he added. By the way, do you have a passport? he asked. I don't, Maria Alexandra responded, but I've been meaning to get one for months. Do that as soon as possible, he said as if in passing, but seriously, you don't know when you may need one. Bogoljub is, in fact, a very old-fashioned name, he told her. When someone in my country says they are named Bogoljub you imagine an eighty-year-old. It's the same as if someone were to be named Suetonius or Horace, he said, and Maria Alexandra laughed. Tito was still alive at the time, and my parents thought that by placing their love of God in their son's name they would be fighting the system. As if the system would suffer from that and not their child, she said. When I started school half of the kids laughed at me, not because of the meaning of my name but because it was so old fashioned. I chose my own nickname—Boško, he said. This is my most terrifying secret, everything else will be much easier to admit.

He spoke about his high-school days, about his graduation trip to Spain. Where will you go on your graduation trip? he asked. There has been some talk about going to Italy, Maria Alexandra said, but I'm not sure if my grandma would let me go, because of the money and all. She shouldn't deny you this, it's once in a lifetime, Boško said. He told her about his studies. There were some difficult days, but about that some other time. I graduated in sociology and became an assistant. I'm here on a research trip, as you know, he said. Yes, Maria Alexandra said, you told me that already but I seem to be the object of your research, she said. Then she paused, and added, Bogoljub. When you address me so officially I'm forced to treat you officially. Call me Boško. In my region they say: business is business, and friendship is friendship. I don't know, remarked Maria Alexandra, it's getting hard to call you by your nickname.

While she lived in Cahul, when she was only twelve or thirteen, Maria Alexandra read in a book that women like to call their beloved by their real name and not by their nickname. She had never thought about this before, but it seemed true. It also seemed she was falling in love with Boško, Bogoljub.

Whenever she said Bogoljub, he clearly showed her that it bothered him. I'm not bothered by the meaning of the name, I don't like the sound of it, all those syllables sound too horrible. One afternoon, however, when they met after school, Maria Alexandra said: You know, Bogoljub, here in high school, we don't only have philosophy but Latin language too. I translated your name into Latin, she said. I'll call you Amadeus. Hey, that sounds good, he said, better than Theophilus. Mozart too, must have translated his name into Latin. She nodded. Do you know the story about Theophilus? he asked. Which Theophilus? Maria Alexandra was quick to ask. The one and only, Boško responded.

You know, Boško began, Theophilus was actually the first Faust, pre-Faust, so to speak. Theophilus is the first man who sold his soul to the devil. It seems a bit ironic. This is a Jacobean story, a story about temptation, temptation to which the protagonist succumbed. You know, Boško continued, the worst curse in my country goes like this: may you have and then have not! That was what happened to poor Theophilus. He sold his soul to the devil in order to get his luck back. For seven years he lived a fine and pleasant enough life, even though the remorse was killing him. He didn't dare to beg God for forgiveness. He prayed to the Mother of God, and she forgave him. Women saved him. I like that story, said Boško finally.

She started calling him Theophilus, which he didn't mind. She tried calling him Amadeus a couple of times but that didn't work. It sounded too funny. I don't associate the name Amadeus with Mozart, it actually reminds me of a silly song from my childhood. Maria Alexandra nevertheless thought about him as Amadeus. Mozart's arias sung by Maria Cebotari were the sonic preludes to her falling in love, a sign of fate.

At first she was happy that Boško didn't try to kiss her. Grandma's tirades against evil men who want only one thing influenced her more than she was willing to admit. As the days grew warmer and spring wore on, as the school year approached its end, his restraint began to worry her. Maybe he doesn't like me, she sometimes thought at night, and then she recalled his look, his smile, his voice, and she knew, she simply knew that he liked her. She found different theories in her head, believed in them, and rejected them, from night to night. One evening all this was resolved.

It was the end of April and there was a performance for the Day of the School. Grandma knew the performance lasted until eight. You must be home by eight-thirty, she said, and Maria Alexandra could hardly hold in her joy. She wouldn't go to the school performance, she thought. She would spend the whole day with Boško.

He kissed her for the first time under an ash tree in the park. He kissed her softly and slowly. He went with the tip of his tongue to the inner side of her teeth, he touched her gently with his teeth before their tongues crashed. They kissed for a long time, until the shadow of the tree melted with the dusk. Afterward they walked holding hands.

I like it that you call me Theophilus, Boško said. It should be like that because you saved me. I sold my soul to the Devil, a female Devil. Her name was Magdalene, he said, but she preferred Magda. She liked me to suffer, he said, and I suffered until I met you. I suffered for seven years.

I met her in high school and I fell in love; I was crazy about her. She wasn't a beauty, he confessed, but she had an aura about her. She was like a heroine from Dostoevsky, a heroine who was all his fatal women in one, he said. At first she was somewhat in love with me, but that time of naïveté lasted for about three months. She started acting capriciously, he said, paying attention to other men, but she didn't leave me. Every month or two she told me she loved me and all other men were around her because of her boredom. Yes, Magda was always bored. She toyed with me in this manner for about four years, and then she became bored of playing. I couldn't get over her for a few years, until you came along.

They kissed again, this time more affectionately and more

passionately. Maria Alexandra could barely tear herself away at a quarter past eight. We have to rush, she said. They almost ran, but every now and then they stopped to kiss. I love you, he said when they were parting. I love you too, she said. She kissed him and headed toward Grandma's house. Maria Alexandra, he called her. She turned around. I am returning to Dubrovnik in twenty days, he said. She was quiet for a moment, stared at his eyes, and then ran to the door.

I'm going with Boško, she said to herself. She almost didn't sleep that whole night. The following day he waited for her at the same spot where they had parted yesterday. Will you come with me? he asked, and Maria Alexandra rushed into his arms.

They agreed about everything that very same morning. She didn't go to school that day but Boško didn't mind it this time. This is more important, and you're basically done with school. I'm leaving on the eighteenth of May. When does your class go on the excursion? he asked. On the thirtieth, she responded. Great, that's just twelve days, he said and kissed her. Where exactly in Italy are you going? he asked in between kisses. Rimini, Maria Alexandra mumbled those three syllables, the sweetest syllables, as another kiss was about to happen. Perfect, Boško said, perfect, that's only an hour and a half by train from Ancona.

Their arrangement was simple. They quickly agreed on everything because Boško had clearly thought about it all, like a real man, thought Maria Alexandra. On the last day of her excursion she would travel from Rimini to Ancona, and Boško would wait for her at the station. They would go together to Dubrovnik. Bring your report cards, Boško said, in case you don't have your diploma yet. You can study in Dubrovnik, there is an excellent university in Dubrovnik where classes are taught in English. We solved it all. Maria Alexandra thought, the only thing is to talk Grandma into letting me go on the trip. As if he read her mind: let Grandma know how much you care about this excursion, be polite and decent, explain to her that everyone is going and that this is a celebration of the successful end of your studies. Now that I'm old enough, I can run away, said Maria Alexandra irascibly. No, Boško said, this is your grandma, be good to her. You'll call her when we get to Dubrovnik and explain everything, the main thing now is for things to happen smoothly.

Grandma told her to take good care of herself but did not object. She gave her money for the trip and a bit extra for pocket money, as she said. At the beginning of May Maria Alexandra gave her teacher the money for the trip and her passport for a visa.

They counted the days until Boško's departure, but there wasn't too much sorrow in the counting. Maria Alexandra was to remain in Chisinau for twelve more days, then be two or three days on the road, and seven days in Rimini. Afterward, at the station in Ancona, she would see Boško and they would not part ways again.

On the seventeenth of May in the afternoon Boško walked her home and quickly said goodbye: see you in Ancona. She was happy the way it all happened. She didn't want to cry in front of him.

So much had accumulated in her heart. The happiness about Boško, her apprehension and anxiety about the trip, about leaving, and sorrow, her old sorrow, for Grandma and the anniversary of her father's passing. After Boško left she paid more attention to her grandma, poor grandma, who was hiding her infinite sorrow behind her care for Maria Alexandra. Something profound ties me to my grandma, Maria Alexandra thought. We share our sorrow.

Apart from her clothes and toiletries, she put only the mirror in her bag, her oval mirror, and the postcard of Dubrovnik.

Early on the morning on the thirtieth of May she said a quick goodbye to her grandma. She didn't want to be too sentimental this time either. Little pricks of conscience were there, nevertheless. I will write her a letter, a long letter, she thought on the bus.

4

Dear Grandma,

Don't worry. That's the main thing. Don't be upset. I'm happy. Try to be happy for me.

I promised to tell you about the trip, about Italy. Everything I've seen from the bus I've been telling you in my thoughts. The trip is long, Europe is big. When you travel from Moldova to Italy it's like looking at a box of children's crayons assembled from black to white: the more westward you go the less darkness and more light you find.

It's different here, the sky is bluer. Dad used to talk about a philosopher who wrote that happiness begins with Vienna. Only now am I able to understand that. The more you go eastward the more unhappiness you find. Even unhappiness has degrees.

Under the gray sky the houses are gray, the people are gray, it's all gray. There is no grayness here. You can find everything here but grayness. The people are strange, as if they miss that grayness a little.

I miss you, Grandma, but I know we'll see each other again. When you know you'll see someone again, whenever that may be, the pain is less. Today I'll see B. As soon as I write this letter and send it I'll head toward the train.

Had I not met him I'd never have overcome the longing for Dad, whom I'll never see again.

The journey has been long, long and difficult. We slept in the bus too. We were stopped and searched by the different customs officials several times. We were tired, anxious, hot. I felt nauseous, I sweated, but one image has driven all of that away. The sea! Seen in the morning, early at dawn, with a few white sails and a blazing red ball at the horizon—postcard kitsch, I know—but irresistible. The scent is different here too, the scent of life. It's a cliché but it feels as if it was taken from a biology textbook. (Life sprang up from under the aegis of the sea!)

Ever since I first saw the sea I haven't moved my face from the window. I think I finally understand the Japanese tourists who always click their cameras. I wanted to remember every image: small stone squares, little ports in the bay, ancient graveyards, olive groves, and vineyards. And people: dark-haired, dark-skinned, cheerful, resembling B, except that B is more handsome. My skin is so pale, I thought, and now (while I'm writing this) it already became slightly reddish, at least on my arms. The skin will accommodate. It's not a problem to accommodate to good things.

We finally reached the hotel. The hotel is called Sole. This is the first hotel I've ever been to. O Sole Mio, I've been singing to myself these days. I'm writing to you from the hotel. I'm by myself in the room. I share it with Helen but I'm by myself now. We mostly miss each other these days: she usually arrives just to go to bed and I'm getting ready for breakfast.

My window overlooks the sea. I spend a lot of time by the window, looking at the sea, trying to see what's across it, on the other side. In vain. At the horizon the two blue spheres join together.

Rimini is ugly. It would better suit Moldova than Italy. If Moldova were sunny and rich, I mean. I find Rimini ugly, I should say, because the rest of the class is actually enjoying it. There are plenty of bars and discotheques and that's what matters to them. Only five or six of us come when we go on day trips. The rest of them sleep.

These day trips have been the best of what I have experienced here. We went to Venice, Florence, Ravenna. I wish B were with me. I'll have to talk him into having us visit these places together. He'll have so much to show me, but I'll be able to take him to my favorite places as well.

There is a church in Venice that I find more beautiful than all the others. It is right by the entrance to Canal Grande—Santa Maria della Salute. Our teacher told us that we shouldn't spend time in this church, that this church isn't considered to be one of the masterpieces, he said. It's somewhat kitschy and asymmetrical but it was imprinted in my memory precisely for those reasons. And because of its name as well. A bit earlier we walked by the Embankment of the Incurables. The teacher mentioned that it got

*its name long ago when the plague swept across Europe. I felt some-
what melancholy about this until I saw the church dedicated to Our
Lady of Health. B told me about the sinner, the deadly sinner, the
incurable one whom Our Lady saved. That's what I remembered.
We spent almost an entire day in Venice, we walked and walked
and I didn't get tired. It was already night when we came back.
At the door of the room I ran into Helen. You're back from Venice,
and I am off to have the time of my life, she said. How unusual,
I thought, to equate life with loud music, inarticulate dance, and
toxins. Life is sometimes more insignificant than life.*

*The next day we went to Ravenna. I always imagined it would
be a city of ravens. Dante's grave is there, which romanticizes it.
How strange to arrive in Ravenna. At first, the city seems indus-
trial, as if it were somewhere in the East. Chimneys, factories, oil
refineries. That was my impression as we entered the city by bus. In
Ravenna itself you are immediately reminded of Venice. Venice is
the past of Ravenna, Ravenna is perhaps the future of Venice. This
was also a city on the water. The sea withdrew and the canals were
filled. The churches in Ravenna, the teacher said, resemble those of
Byzantium. This place is the East in the West, I thought. It's just
that heaviness replaced the lightness: earth instead of water. There
were many Japanese tourists with cameras, but here I saw something
I haven't seen before. It was a very hot day. Three Japanese men who
stood by the church snapping their cameras wore baseball hats. It
was not the hats that were strange, strange were the fans installed
on them, fans that supposedly run on solar energy. That is progress:
from solar calculator to ventilator.*

*We have a fan here in the hotel room. It works on electricity but
hardly helps at all. The weather is awfully hot. I could use a walk
by the sea. The wind, the real wind, blows lightly, tousles my hair
and cools my face. That's how I spent the evening when we returned
from Ravenna: I walked by myself at the shore. Some idle men
called after me, but I ignored them. I thought about B. He doesn't
shout after women like this, he's not like this, I'm sure.*

I wish you had met B but I didn't dare to introduce him to you. I know you well enough: you'd have gotten rid of him. It doesn't matter. You will meet him one day. You can't get rid of him anymore. He is on his way to meet me. I'm getting ready to meet with him. Today is the day I have been waiting for. I'm counting the hours.

We had no day trips for the next two days. I had stayed in Rimini. I explored the town, looked for solitary streets. I spent this time alone.

I've been thinking: you already know this! You will actually know it all before you get this letter. When they go back to Chisinau, when they arrive without me, they'll say I acted strangely all this time, I was by myself often, I didn't have a good time, and didn't go out with others. She has been strange ever since she came to our class, they'll say. Helen may say: she always looked toward the open sea. They'll probably insinuate that I killed myself, that I drowned. They'll speak about my sorrow, solitude, depression. The teachers will apologize, bow down before you begging for your forgiveness, at least they did everything they could to help me integrate into the community and to get over the family tragedy. But you'll know, I know you'll know, that I didn't go to Italy to kill myself. You'll worry, you already worry about unplanned things. You fear trouble, misfortune, disaster. Don't worry, Grandma.

On a deserted street, at a stony window, I saw an older woman who reminded me of you, she looked like your twin sister. She was watering flowers. I don't know why, but I was sure she lived by herself. I started crying to myself, Grandma. The woman looked at me kindly, the way you looked at me at parting, and I knew you'd understand.

The next day, as I walked around, I found a graveyard. I entered it. I sought solitude. It was empty, not a living soul there. I walked slowly and whispered out the names on the crosses. The straight carved letters reminded me of a computer font, "Times New Roman." What a silly association, I thought, I even smiled. I was smiling joyously until I saw a bunch of wilted flowers on a grave. Someone had brought it two or three days ago, brought it for someone who was their own, someone dead. I left quickly.

The next day, during our trip to Florence, I didn't want to go see the graves of Michelangelo, Galileo, Rossini. One shouldn't go to a grave for vanity's sake. The art teacher was surprised: You like cultural education, he said. These were living people, living, like you and I, and not some names in bold from dusty books, I wanted to say that but I didn't.

I have a favorite church in Florence, only my choice here is very predictable. Everyone likes the Florence Cathedral. It's called Santa Maria del Fiore. I remembered the bucket with the wilted flowers from yesterday. What is it in people, I thought, what is it in me precisely, to think that everything in the world, even things that happened long ago, someone's intimate sorrows, have something to do with me?

More students came on the trip to Florence than to Venice or Ravenna. Someone said that young people love Florence. At dusk Helen took me to a street with jewelry shops. Their windows were flashier than the Japanese cameras. Helen sighed. I thought about my mirror, which was more precious to me than all of Florence. I thought about the ring B would give me one day. It wouldn't be gold and wouldn't have precious stones. Silver would be best. It's not exactly bijouterie, but its value is not in money. On the return the bus dropped us off at the hotel, but Helen didn't even come to the room. She followed the golden shine of the neon signs to the nightclubs.

I didn't sleep well that night. It crossed my mind that I was possibly missing something by not going with Helen. The soul is weak in the dark of the night.

We had a trip to Verona scheduled for the next day. This time everyone wanted to go. It's because of Romeo and Juliet, whispered the psychology teacher. I didn't want to go to Verona. I'm not attracted by the romanticism of unrealized love. I said to Helen that I had a stomachache.

Actually, I had a headache, because of poor sleep. It wasn't bad enough to prevent me from traveling, though. I didn't want to listen to my classmates' affectations about true love that exists only in movies, while in reality one needs to take everything life has to offer. I was even less interested in the dull humor of the clumsy boys who went to the excursion in hopes of taking advantage of the drunken girls.

I lay in my room until late afternoon. Afterward, I went for a walk. I went to the shore but the sea wasn't very clear. Then, I saw a cinema on one street. I approached the door. The poster announced the feature film. On the poster, in large print, was my name, or half of my name, Maria Full of Grace, was the title. The poster showed the picture of a girl, black hair, beautiful, my age. Under the poster, on a blue ribbon, there was the schedule of the showings. The first one was starting in half an hour.

There were ten people in the audience altogether. The room was small yet big enough for all of us to enjoy solitude. I sat in the middle of the next-to-last row. The movie was in Spanish, subtitled into Italian, but that didn't bother me. The storyline was simple. I could concentrate on the faces. The face of Maria, Maria from Colombia, reminded me of my face, of the reflection of my face in my precious mirror. Maria works with flowers in Colombia, she strips thorns from the roses, the roses meant for rich Western flower shops. I remembered the Florence Cathedral from yesterday, Santa Maria del Fiore. Maria goes North, the North is her West, and westward is where happiness is. She has to pay for that happiness. The price is mercy, the price is drugs. And in her, another life is beginning.

I left the cinema, and for the first time in Italy I was afraid. The sea is just an image, and beauty is an image, the summer, the flowers. Somewhere underneath the sea there must be life, and in life there is pain. Maria from Colombia strips thorns from roses, the sick call for help from Our Lady of Health. This is a terrifying world, I thought, it's good that I have B. I knew that I'd see him the next day.

I'll be off, Grandma, it's time. Forgive me. Be happy for me if you can. We'll meet again sometime, somewhere.

I'm going to see B. He is waiting for me, I know he is waiting for me. My thoughts are already with him, so I will end this letter.

Today we'll see each other and go together and be together. B is
taking me to the East, a little bit to the East, but it's as if we are
going to the West.
  Farewell Grandma, farewell!
  Love,
  Yours,
  (Maria) Alexandra

5

She had the stamps and the envelope ready. Maria Alexandra
licked the edge of the envelope, packed the letter, and left the
room. She didn't take much clothing, only the underwear that
could fit in her purse. That's what Boško told her to do. We're
beginning a new life, he said, you don't need anything from the
old one. In her bag she had her passport, student card, wallet,
mirror, and the letter for her grandma.

In front of the hotel there was a mailbox into which she threw
her letter. Afterward she headed straight for the station. During
her first day in Rimini she found the station and bought the
train ticket right then and there, as she had agreed with Boško.
The ticket was in her wallet for a week. Not a day passed that
Maria Alexandra didn't look at it. She saw a code for her future
in the letters of departure and destination cities, in the numerals
of the time and date.

She arrived at the platform early. She couldn't be late, by no
means. Those minutes before the train arrived were terribly long.
Since Boško left Chisinau the time hasn't passed that slowly. She
was nervous, biting the skin around her nails, she paced back and
forth. As soon as she entered the car, she settled down. When the
train left the station, she felt relieved. It's over now, it's over. She
observed the landscape through the window. It was beautiful but
not magical as she had thought seven, eight days ago when she
saw Italy for the first time through the dusty plexiglass. Nothing

is like the first time, thought Maria Alexandra. Then she smiled and blushed timidly.

The train entered the station and her eyes sought Boško. She didn't see him through the window but as soon as she stepped onto the platform he appeared beside her. He gave her a hug, a strong one, without words, and then kissed her. I envisioned this differently, she whispered, I thought I'd see you from fifty meters ahead, we'd be running toward each other. You watch too many movies, he said, but, if you wish, we can do this again. He rushed to the other end of the platform. Maria Alexandra looked at him in awe. He turned and, with his eyes wide open, ran toward her. She smiled and moved toward him. They hugged. He said: there, you had your cinematic encounter. I saw an excellent movie yesterday, she said. You'll tell me about it, Boško interrupted her, let's first get something to eat.

The restaurant was near the sea. They sat at one of the tables, on a big terrace. Boško ordered a bottle of wine. What do you feel like eating? he asked. Some pasta, said Maria Alexandra, with seafood. Excellent, Boško was pleased, something light with white wine so you don't get seasick. Tonight we're taking the ferry to Split, he said. Tomorrow we'll be there, and then we'll be off to Dubrovnik.

The waiter brought the plates. Maria Alexandra spoke about the movie she had seen, but she noticed that Boško wasn't listening attentively. She stopped. Go on, Boško said, tell me, forgive me, I was paying attention less to the story and more to your voice. He half-stood, leaned toward her, and kissed her.

After they finished their meal they continued to sip the wine. Ancona is an ugly town, Boško said, it's better if we sit here until it's time to go to the port. The Sun was setting slowly. This is a perfect image of happiness, Maria Alexandra thought. Boško behaved as if he knew what she was thinking. The summer sunset at the Mediterranean, being in love, wine, is the most beautiful thing in the world, he said, even though my colleagues from the university would certainly say this is all kitsch. What do they know, smiled Maria Alexandra.

Boško ordered another bottle of wine. Maria Alexandra felt that the drink was loosening her up. We'll be alone tonight in the cabin, she thought, our first time alone the entire night. She had a big sip of wine and shut her eyes. She envisioned the swinging of the cabin, the night, the waves. It will be warm and stuffy, Boško's body will be hot and slippery, she'll be intoxicated and happy. Her knees were trembling with excitement. It was perfect.

The glasses were empty. Boško poured the last drops of wine from the bottle. He looked at his watch. Let's drink this and go, he said. They clinked their glasses. For you, Boško said. For us, Maria Alexandra said.

I rented a cabin, if you get sleepy, Boško said while they were getting on the ferry. A twin-bed cabin, he added after a short pause. Maria Alexandra didn't say a thing. She wanted to say that one bed would do, it was on the tip of her tongue, so to speak, but she didn't say it.

The night is mild, let's sit on the deck for a while, whispered Boško. Sure, she responded. The ship was slowly making its way out of the harbor. The people on deck were mostly looking at the lights of Ancona, toward the shore. Maria Alexandra stared into the darkness on the other side, gazing at the other shore, which wasn't yet in sight.

She was glad that Boško hadn't been aggressive with her back in Chisinau. She knew what men could be like—from books and from Grandma's stories. She knew, however, what her dad was like. If Boško weren't different she would have never fallen in love with him. If he had cared about only one thing, as Grandma said, she'd have been rid of him a long time ago. Now, she wanted what she had earlier feared. She still feared it, but her desire was much stronger.

She snuggled up to Boško. They sat on a bench at the top of the deck. It was quiet. The only sound was the motor running. I love you, Boško, Maria Alexandra said. I love you too, Boško whispered while kissing her ear. I'm ready, she said quietly. I know, Boško mumbled, not lifting his mouth from her lips. Maria Alexandra shuddered. A new type of cramp stroked her entire body. I'll bring us more wine, Boško said, it's too early to go to the cabin, the evening has just begun.

They drank the wine on the deck. Maria Alexandra wasn't sure if she was dizzy because she was seasick, or because she drank, or from desire and happiness. Suddenly, like at the end of childhood, the tiredness came over her. She wanted to stay awake but her eyes were closing on their own. She even took a brief nap on the deck. Boško woke her up gently. She leaned on him and they went slowly to the cabin. She undressed quickly, went to bed, and covered herself. Before she fell asleep, in a half-dream, she saw Boško getting into the other bed. The rounded light from the lamp covered his face. He stretched his arm, pressed the switch, and turned the lamp off. Sleep came with the darkness.

Maria Alexandra woke up early. Boško was still asleep. Occasional snoring came from his bed, probably what had woken her. The sound wasn't pleasant, but it moved her. That's love, she thought, when you like the ugly things about the person you love. It was then that a strange thought passed through her head. Will I like his snoring in twenty years? she wondered. I will, she thought quickly to shake off the doubt. But the thought returned. She got up. Quickly and quietly she dressed. She tiptoed over to Boško's bed and stared at his sleeping face. He was frowning. She discerned dark bristles on his cheeks and his chin, which had seemed smooth last night. The sleepy body started to toss around as if he felt her gaze. She didn't want to wake him. She left the room in silence and closed the door.

As she was going out onto the deck she thought about sleep and sleeplessness. To care for the sleep of a loved one, to watch a person and not wake him, that is something inseparable from love. Her dad liked to cite a philosopher who wrote that the happiest moment of the happiest man is the moment when he falls asleep, and the unhappiest moment of the unhappiest man is when he wakes up. She never opposed her dad, but she didn't think this was true. Ever since she had begun to love Boško, ever since she was with him, she hadn't liked sleeping. It's similar to the song: he doesn't want to close his eyes, he doesn't want to fall asleep because she'll miss him, because he doesn't want to miss a moment they may spend together. Yet it was strange that despite everything she didn't want to wake him.

She was sitting on the deck thinking and paying no attention to anything else. When she got up she saw the outline of the Dalmatian coast on the horizon. The morning freshness slowly gave way to June heat. Maria Alexandra stared at the coast. That's where she'd live from now on, she thought. She was able to recognize the whiteness of the city. Split, she whispered to herself. And then she heard the steps. She hadn't yet turned when she heard the voice too. There you are, early riser, said Boško brightly.

We'll be there soon, he said after a long morning kiss. Where is your passport, he asked. Downstairs, in the cabin, she said. Let me have it, Boško replied, I'll show them both at customs. My acquaintance is on duty this morning, he promised not to hold us back, he added.

They kissed on the deck. After each kiss Split got closer and closer. First they saw the buildings, and then the windows on the buildings, and then the palms in front of them. They were nearing the harbor. Wait for me here, Boško said, I'll go downstairs to pick up our stuff.

He was back fast. I took your passport. It was sticking out from the bag. It's not possible that it was sticking out, she thought, but that didn't matter. Boško is a man, a real man, the one who likes to have everything under his control, she told herself.

The ship came in to shore slowly. They disembarked in no time. Boško showed the two passports. The young man grinned and said something in a language she didn't understand. They were already on the ground, at the port. The unpleasant smell of the port was Maria Alexandra's first impression of Split. Who cares for first impressions, she thought. Let's go for a coffee, Boško said. All of a sudden he seemed different, as if the touch of his homeland brought him some strange peace, almost coldness. They sat in a big outdoor café by the water. Across from them was a line of palms and white benches. It was crowded, both in the café and on the waterfront. Boško chatted with the waiter, and then started reading the newspaper. It was unusual to hear Boško speak a language she didn't understand. She tried to draw him into conversation but he was absent. He read the paper and every now and then glanced at his watch. He turned his cell phone on and placed it by his cigarette pack.

The phone rang, Boško spoke briefly, and afterward he cheered up. That was my friend, he said, he'll come in the afternoon to pick us up and drive us to Dubrovnik. We can take the bus too, Maria Alexandra said. It's too hot for the bus, and besides it's awfully crowded, Boško responded, it's better like this. Let's go, I'll show you around.

Finally, Maria Alexandra managed to relax a little. She was having a nice time. They had breakfast at McDonald's, and for dessert a banana split in a cake shop. When I was a boy I thought the dessert was named after Split, Boško said, and Maria Alexandra laughed. He showed her the palace of the Roman imperator Diocletian and a monument to a bishop with a raised finger. They walked the entire morning. They took a break to enjoy ice cream at one of the white benches right across the café where they had had coffee earlier that morning. Only a few hours had passed but that seemed so long ago.

Later they walked more aimlessly and stopped for lunch at a restaurant. Boško had fish, Maria Alexandra pizza. Boško ordered wine. The cell phone rang again, the conversation was brief. Our driver will meet us in half an hour, Boško said, I mean the friend of mine who is taking us to Dubrovnik.

First she saw Boško waving to someone, and then she turned around herself. A man in dark-green Bermuda shorts and blue shirt with a sign Maria Alexandra couldn't understand approached their table. He had a long beard and stank of sweat. My name is Ljubo, he said in a barely comprehensible English, offering his sticky palm.

Ljubo ordered lunch. The waiter brought an enormous platter with mixed meat and potatoes. He kept offering Maria Alexandra to join him, gesturing with his finger, even though she told him clearly that she had just eaten. She even asked Boško to translate this for him. Boško completely devoted his attention to Ljubo. The two of them talked in their own language, they laughed, drank, and clinked their glasses. They poured drinks for Maria Alexandra, but she tried not to drink too much. I don't like Ljubo, she thought, but he is Boško's friend. We'll get better acquainted, she thought, there is time.

They sat at the restaurant for a long time. It was dusk when they left the restaurant and walked toward Ljubo's car. Maria Alexandra sat in the back. As soon as Ljubo started the car he played some cheerful music. I can't wait to get to Dubrovnik, to Boško's, our, home. Music was playing loudly, Boško and Ljubo were shouting to each other. Maria Alexandra leaned her head against the window and shut her eyes. Even if she didn't fall asleep, she'd doze off a bit.

It was already night when she opened her eyes. She looked for the sea but didn't see it. Is Dubrovnik close? she asked Boško. We'll stay here for the night, before we head to Dubrovnik, Boško said. Afterward he said something to Ljubo and Ljubo laughed.

They stopped by a big three-story house. Above the door there was a sign: *Night Club*. Maria Alexandra was confused. There was music coming from the house, similar to the music Ljubo was playing in the car.

They entered a large, semi-dark, and very smoky room. There was only one woman inside. She was dancing around a metal bar, dressed only in lace panties.

The three of them sat at a table. Boško, Maria Alexandra called him, Boško, but he ignored her. As she tried to get up, Ljubo roughly pushed her back. Two more men came to their table and looked at her the way one looks at a cake in a cake shop: with mouth half opened and hungry eyes. They all laughed. Another woman came from somewhere. One of the men said something to her, and the woman asked Maria Alexandra to follow her.

They walked toward the stairs. Maria Alexandra felt the looks on the back of her head. The woman told her something but Maria Alexandria didn't understand.

Upstairs, about ten women gathered around her. They talked but didn't laugh. One thin girl asked her: how are you? Maria Alexandra's eyes filled with tears for a moment when she realized she was standing before a girl from her country. I am Sonja, she said, and gave her a hug. Her response was barely audible due to the sobbing: I am Maria Alexandra.

They entered a room with a big bed. There was nothing else in the room. Through tears, Maria Alexandra told her everything. Everything. You are a virgin, Sonja said, they brought you for the general. Two months ago they brought a Ukrainian girl, Julia. She was with us until ten days ago. They sold her to Serbia. The general pays for the virgins, Sonja said, he pays a lot for a night or two. Afterward everyone else takes advantage of her. At least this is how it happened with Julia, she said while stroking Maria Alexandra's hair.

Steps were heard from the stairs. A man's voice, then a woman's. The woman who had brought Maria Alexandra upstairs entered the room and said something to Sonja. Sonja said: take a bath, the general is coming tonight.

In the bathroom there was only a shallow bathtub and a small white cabinet with red panties lying on it. There was no mirror. Maria Alexandra turned the water on, but she didn't take off her clothes. She sat down at the edge of the bathtub and stared at the big yellow ceramic tiles on the wall across from her. She stared at the wall for two or three minutes and then took the gift Dad gave her for her fourth birthday from the purse. My little mirror, she whispered. She let the water come louder, and then she approached the wall and broke the mirror. It broke into three pieces. The top part of the largest piece was as sharp as a diamond. She cut the veins on her left arm. She cut forcefully, vigorously, effectively. She didn't feel any pain. The blood flowed everywhere. She continued to slice her arm upward to the elbow. Before she lost consciousness, she made one cut across her throat.

Maria Alexandra died on the eighth of June 2004, on the day of Venus's transit across the Sun.

ECLIPSE

A writer ought to write and build a story,
not make his life into a story.

Ivo Andrić: *Signs by the Roadside.*

One

THE WRITER WAS BORN in Dubrovnik. He was very glad about this fact even though it was all just coincidence. It may be that coincidence itself that he was actually glad about.

I was supposed to give birth at the end of June, his mother told him on numerous occasions. I was really impossible during pregnancy, she said, so your father tried to brighten me up by taking me to Dubrovnik for a weekend. We stayed at the best hotel, The Argentina. It wasn't too expensive as it was out of season. We arrived around noon. I was just about to take a shower when my water broke. Commotion, panic, the hospital. I was in labor for a long time, she said, and the Writer tried not to imagine that scene. I know, I know it very well, that's how the story usually ended, that I gave birth to you just before midnight. First came you and then a few moments later—the bells.

The Writer's birth certificate said he was born on the nineteenth of May. His mother, on the other hand, claimed that he was born on the eighteenth. Who cares, Dad would say, one minute more or less, it's not as if you were giving birth on the thirty-first of December, when that one minute would determine the year of his birth. Eighteenth or nineteenth—it doesn't really matter, even his horoscope sign remains the same, he said triumphantly. He's a Taurus regardless.

The Writer thought that way for a long time. What my birth certificate says is what matters, he said to himself. What's important is that I was born in Dubrovnik, he thought, that's what makes me different from others in the class. All his friends from school were mostly born in Travnik, where they lived. The exceptions were the kids whose fathers were in the military.

They, however, came from towns with gloomy and unattractive names. Not him. He was from Dubrovnik. That is what mattered, not the birthday. Some kids were born during the break, either summer or winter break, some of the kids' birthdays fell on Republic Day or Youth Day, but that meant nothing. All days are the same. One is the same as any other. All cities, however, are not the same.

This all changed in the seventh grade, with an issue of *Male Novine*, a children's newspaper. The topic was famous Yugoslavs. The language teacher remarked that among famous Yugoslavs was one, Ivo Andrić, from their town. One of my fellow townsmen is there as well, the Writer noted: Ruđer Bošković.

Looking at the pictures of Bošković, Andrić, Tesla, Pupin, Prelog, Ružička, Krleža, and Tito, the Writer paid little attention to their birthdays, only to birthplace. When he came home after school that day, he carefully read the short biographies of all eight famous Yugoslavs. This time he considered their birthdays carefully. When he saw Bošković's birthday he raised his eyebrows in surprise. He left the paper on his bed and went to the living room. Mom and Dad were drinking coffee. Mom, when is my birthday? asked the Writer. What do you want for your birthday? asked Dad smiling. Mom, when is my birthday? he repeated. In three months, Mom responded. When exactly? asked the Writer more loudly. It says on your report card, his dad answered. When was I born, Mom? asked the Writer, on the eighteenth or on the nineteenth of May? Come on, Son, Dad responded with irritation, we've spoken about this hundreds of times. Your birthday is on the nineteenth, as it says on your birth certificate. Mom? asked the Writer imploringly. Dad told you nicely, Mom said, it says in your papers that you were born on the nineteenth of May, even though I'm sure that I had you on the eighteenth. But what's the use of that since my own husband and my own child don't believe me. I believe you, Mommy, said the Writer. He kissed his mom on the cheek and went back to his room. He focused again on one word and a few digits underneath it. Ruđer Bošković was born in Dubrovnik on the eighteenth of May, the Writer said out loud, as if to convince himself.

Two years later, when he was already in high school, the Writer found a book in the library, which linked all the days of the year to famous people born on each day. On the nineteenth of May, his official birthday, the following people were born: the German philosopher Fichte, the Turkish president Mustafa Kemal Atatürk, the American political activist Malcolm X. On the eighteenth of May, on his actual birthday, the philosopher, writer, and Nobel Prize winner Bertrand Russell was born, as well as the director Frank Capra, architect Walter Gropius, and, of course, Ruđer Bošković. Then, the Writer didn't know much about Fichte. He only remembered reading somewhere about certain nationalistic speeches this philosopher had made during Napoleonic conquests. Such a philosopher, who is more a politician than a philosopher, shares his birthday with two other politicians. So the nineteenth is a day when politicians were born. The eighteenth, on the other hand, is a day for artistic birthdays, thought the Writer. I was definitely born on the eighteenth. The Writer already knew that he was going to become a writer.

In the next few years the Writer read more than ever. He was learning his craft, and besides, there was a war. One neighborhood kid had changed his name during the war years. The Writer was interested in a possible political reason for a name change. He was interested to know if it was possible to change one's date of birth. He once asked his mom about this, but she just smiled. Don't invest this with so much significance, she said. It's easy to say that, thought the Writer.

When it came to celebrating his birthday he found a solution. He organized his parties on the evening of the eighteenth under the pretext that they would wait for midnight, that is, his birthday, the way one welcomes the New Year. His friends were convinced. He was an eccentric, an artistic type, and everyone expected such extravagances from him. When at midnight everyone wished him a happy birthday he was always smiling strangely. It's not that we are welcoming my birthday but seeing it off, he thought.

It was only after the war that the Writer accepted the nineteenth of May as his official birthday. It was all due to a book—Auster's *The New York Trilogy*. At the beginning, or almost the beginning of the book, which would become his favorite, was written: "It was May nineteenth. He would remember the date because it was his parents' anniversary—or would have been, had his parents been alive—and his mother had once told him that he had been conceived on her wedding night. This fact had always appealed to him—being able to pinpoint the first moment of his existence—and over the years he had privately celebrated his birthday on that day." If the nineteenth of May can be Daniel Quinn's real birthday, he thought, it can be my birthday as well, my official birthday. The eighteenth of May, via Dubrovnik, ties me to Bošković, thought the Writer, while the nineteenth of May via my birth certificate ties me to Quinn and Auster.

After reading *The New York Trilogy* the Writer knew that he wanted to be a writer. Even before this he had written a poem or two, a few stories, but all these were just an exercise and he didn't try to publish them. I sought my own voice, the Writer thought, and Auster helped me there. It's all connected, it's all one, all is harmony; the chances and coincidences are signs of this harmony. That is what one ought to write about, thought the Writer, but not high-strung and pathetic, no crudeness or cheap cynicism. It should be done the way Auster does it: naturally and in an old-fashioned way. One ought to tell a story, realized the Writer, one's own story but not the story of oneself.

What is my own story? the Writer asked himself, finding no answer. In fact he came up with too many answers, and in their plurality no one answer stood out. He knew, however, what his stories were not. The war was not his story: not as the entrenched apotheosis of masculinity, nor as a sadomasochistic catalog of suffering. The resigned despair of a misfit individual was not his story either: not as a drinking odyssey of a brute with a good soul nor as a litany of the misunderstood intellectual, not as a righteous struggle of one-against-all, nor as a pulpit destroying all before it. He was disgusted by the thought of stories about apartheids and bombastic quasi-autobiographical texts in the first-person singular in which the narrator is the fantasized alter ego of the insecure author, or politically correct onanisms about the penetration of the cultures, the diaspora, or the condition called exile, and politically incorrect masturbations of fat cynics, in which routine, repetitive misanthropy alternates with a sticky and slimy sentimentality.

There was no story, but one had to go on with life. The Writer wrote a short review of Auster's novel *In the Country of Last Things*, which he sent to the editor of a Sarajevo weekly. The review was published. The Writer continued to write about books occasionally. This is what I'll do until I find my story, he thought. Even Auster had written about books before he wrote his own.

From a journalistic perspective, however, books were not particularly attractive subjects. The Writer started publishing articles about film, theater, comic books, pop music, even soccer. If Auster could write about baseball I can do the same about soccer, thought the Writer.

He read a great deal but not as much as before. The newspaper work took a lot of his time. This is just temporary, he consoled himself, until I find my story.

At times, usually late at night, he thought he had found a story. I will write about Shelley's last days, it occurred to him one time. Another time he thought to write a novel with the city of Trieste as its leitmotif: From Italo Svevo to the shopping trips his parents told him about. On a third occasion he thought about insomnia. What kind of subject is that? he asked himself: from the ancient Bosniak by the name of Nespin to Andrić's work from 1937! I will write about Gnostic praise of awakedness, cite Ciorian's bitter aphorisms about insomnia, analyze Borges's troubles with insomnia, thus thought the Writer during his own insomnia, convinced he had finally found his story. He fell asleep before dawn. After he woke up the story evaporated the same way the stories about Shelly and Trieste had evaporated before.

Despite everything he had no doubt that the story would come. Patience. He often thought about a line from Borges: for the first book one has all the time in the world, for the second—far less.

He decided to keep a diary. He feared that his constant writing for the newspapers would damage his style, the style he had built by reading, the style in which he had not yet told the story, his story.

He wrote in his diary about books he had read, but not in a journalistic way, he wrote about rejected ideas, noted effective aphoristic phrases and resonant verses, outlined his meditations. His model for this type of writing was Krleža's diary *Much, Thence Nothing*, a book which Krleža started writing on the Writer's official birthday, the nineteenth of May, 1916.

The diary took him back to Auster. He wanted to write about *The New York Trilogy*, he wanted to shape the sensation invoked by his favorite book with sound words. The new reading made the book even better, but the Writer couldn't write about it. *The New York Trilogy* resisted commentary.

Later he went back to other Auster books. He wrote in his diary about *Mr. Vertigo* and *Leviathan*. It was *Moon Palace*, however, that brought him the story, his story.

Like *The New York Trilogy*, *Moon Palace* improved with each new reading. There was something musical in the way the entire book was permeated by the motif of the moon, with almost infinite manifestations of that motif, from the most trivial to the metaphysical. This time, the Writer didn't finish the entire Auster sonata. At the precise midpoint of the book he saw his story.

In the middle of the book appears one of the main marginal characters: Nikola Tesla. Auster brilliantly sketches Tesla's destiny over a few pages: from the tall man in a white tuxedo at the Chicago World's Fair to the thin, white, old man who feeds pigeons in New York. In the context of the book as a whole this episode is mostly ornamental. It is beautiful and effective but the book could have done without it. The Writer was certain that the hidden purpose of Tesla's presence in *Moon Palace* was actually his, the Writer's story. Auster, with the help of Tesla, pulled the veil from his eyes. He clearly saw his story and the only thing he couldn't figure out was how he hadn't seen it earlier. It was obvious, right from the start.

It was because of Tesla that he remembered that issue of the *Male Novine* about famous Yugoslavs. He remembered the discovery of his real birthday. He remembered Ruđer Bošković. The story about Ruđer Bošković, the Writer noted in his diary, that is my story.

Two

He began his research by leafing through an encyclopedia. That's what he always liked to do: pick a volume, open it at random, and glance through different names and ideas. This time, however, there was nothing random about it. He opened the first volume and amongst Bhagavadita, Bible, Belarus, Bosnia, Bosporus, Boston, and Byzantium, he found Ruđer Bošković (lat. Rogerius Josephus Boshkovich). The encyclopedia entry began with information about the time and the place of birth and death. The entry ended with the Latin titles of Bošković's works. Between the gravestone's digits and their corresponding cities, and his bibliography, there was a condensed biographical sketch: Jesuit, professor of mathematics, astronomer, traveled through Italy and different European countries, helped his native Republic as a diplomat, drew a map of the Pope's state, measured the Rome-Rimini meridian arc with Christian Mayer, achieved admirable results in geophysics, neurology, archeology, wrote poems and travelogues, developed an original theory of force. There is no story here, thought the Writer, no story.

The next step in his investigation was the Internet. Reluctantly, he Googled Ruđer Bošković. He usually used the Internet for journalism, and to lower this story, his story, to the level of journalism made him uneasy. Due to this discomfort the Writer soon gave up the Internet search for Ruđer Bošković. In any event, the first several hits on Google did not refer to the man himself but an institute in Zagreb named after Ruđer Bošković.

The only other source left was the library, where the Writer managed to find a monograph on Ruđer Bošković. I'll read it, he thought, I actually know so little about Bošković, I only know that the story about him is my story as well.

That evening, accompanied by whiskey and cigarettes and quiet music by Mozart, in such a celebratory atmosphere, the Writer began to read Bošković's biography. When he was younger he used to make himself watch a movie or read a book until the very end, even if they were painfully boring, only because they were a part of some canon or were considered cult—an adjective the Writer found despicable. This is how he wasted time on certain French writers and Iranian directors, until he recognized himself in Borges's note on reader's hedonism. After that he'd give a half an hour of time to a boring movie after which he'd take it out of the VCR. He generously gave fifty pages' time to a book that interested him at least a little, otherwise he'd be closing them for good while feeling no guilt. After twenty pages the Bošković monograph was still boring.

What bothered him about the book was the same thing that had bothered him about the entry in the encyclopedia: the absence of a story. The dryness of encyclopedic summary was replaced here by the stiffness of biographical prose burdened by the context and threatened by the grandeur of the subject.

Finally, one detail from the biography put the Writer in a good mood and caused him to smile. Bošković's father had worked in Novi Pazar. In his notebook, the Writer noted: "Ruđer Bošković, son of a jeans smuggler." Enough for tonight, he thought.

The next morning, the first song he heard on the radio was "Total Eclipse of the Heart." He went out for a coffee and on the way there he bought a paper. He lit a cigarette, sipped the hot coffee, and opened the Culture section. The longest text treated the previous day's premier performance of *Eclipse of the Blood.* He didn't pay attention to these hints until he started reading the Bošković monograph in the evening, and stumbled upon a story, or more precisely, a poem, about the eclipse.

First, he found some information about Bošković's teacher Pater Borgondie, who published his observations on the eclipse of the Sun and the Moon viewed from Rome at the end of the third decade of the eighteenth century. This fact didn't quite raise a smile, he didn't think it had anything to do with Bošković. Only a few pages later, however, was the title of a long poem of Bošković's in Latin, a poem whose lines Bošković had written in 1735, a poem whose title the Writer could translate even with his limited high-school knowledge of Latin, *De Solis ac Lunae Defectibus.* A poem about eclipses, the Writer muttered to himself, that's it! In his notebook the Writer jotted down: "Bošković wrote a long poem about the eclipse of the Sun and Moon." Underneath it he added: "Like Lucretius?"

Eclipses, the Writer thought, now that's a story. He recalled his dad telling him about an eclipse he remembered very well. It was winter or early spring of 1961, he told him. I remember that as the year when Ivo Andrić received the Nobel Prize for literature. His dad told him about the eclipse long ago, when the Writer was in fourth or fifth grade, after he had read about eclipses in the book of one thousand questions—one thousand answers. The book explained briefly how the eclipse of the Sun occurs. There was a diagram as well. The article ended with a sentence explaining that a total eclipse of the Sun that is visible from the same point on Earth happens only once in three hundred and sixty years. Dad, do you remember any of the total eclipses of the Sun? the Writer asked him. His dad told him the story of how he and his friends, when they were kids, had watched an eclipse through sooty glass. I will never see an eclipse of the Sun, thought the Writer, encountering a strange sorrow previously unknown to him. He called it a metaphysical sorrow, despite the fact that he didn't quite understand the meaning of the word "metaphysical." He didn't even think that one could see an eclipse anywhere other than in their hometown. I was born too late, or too early, I'll never see an eclipse. Never, he repeated several times, never, he repeated it in his thoughts like a refrain, like the dark bird from a poem he hadn't read yet. Later, months and years later, he thought of this: I'll never see an eclipse. It was only during the war, with the inflation of metaphorical overuse of the notion of eclipse, when every now and then people talked about an eclipse of the mind, sense, and humanity, that the Writer quit thinking about the total eclipse of the Sun. The millennium hysteria over the eclipse almost bypassed him. At that time, in the summer of 1999, the Writer was in America. There was a certain two-month workshop for journalists who work in countries in transition. The Writer followed the news from his homeland over the Internet. Much was written about the eclipse during those August days: the columnists remembered their childhood, conspiracy theorists recalled Nostradamus, experts cautioned people against watching the eclipse with the naked eye, not even through sunglasses, and threatened people with potential blindness. The Writer recalled his father's memories and thought about a time when the world didn't rumble with threats of punishment and dire consequences, a time when there were no flashing warnings on cigarette boxes, a time when freedom implied personal responsibility, a time that may have never existed except in the projection of people who were born afterward. The Writer sat in front of the computer reading the announcements of the eclipse, total or partial, he didn't know, announcements that were printed in capital letters in newspapers from home, and he knew this was confirmation of the most invaluable realization that those two months in America had brought him. He felt this realization powerfully, he felt it deep inside himself, yet he couldn't find a way to express it profoundly to himself or others. Even when he tried the whole matter seemed somehow vague, although it wasn't quite like that. The realization had to do with the importance or realistic judgment about one's own place in the world. In other words, it had to do with an awareness of an incurable megalomania that has always reigned in Bosnia. If there is an eclipse of the Sun in Bosnia and its surroundings, the Writer thought ironically, people there think that the whole world has experienced an eclipse. If they only knew that that eclipse didn't concern anyone in America, he thought, the same way an eclipse visible in America did not concern Europeans. The *Boston Globe* published on the twelfth of August a microscopic line from Budapest mentioning the eclipse. The small article was jammed between the news about sextets born somewhere in Canada and a photograph of the Nigerian minister for foreign affairs. The Writer even wrote a sarcastic review ("Eclipse at Noon") echoing Koestler's title, but the weekly paper didn't publish it.

The eclipse, which he couldn't see from Boston, now reminded him of Boston. He thought of Boston in relation to Bošković even earlier when he was leafing through the encyclopedia. He was thinking about Boston, about Cambridge, about Chestnut Hill, about places where he spent his two American months. The workshop in which he participated took place at Boston College, and the participants were placed with professors. His hostess was Helen. Among all the days within those nine American weeks, among all the people he met, among all the coffee shops, bookstores, squares, libraries, streets, and parks he visited, his thoughts did not look toward Harvard Square with the most beautiful bookstores he had ever seen; he did not think of the campuses on whose paths and lawns ran squirrels by parked bicycles; he did not think of the Charles River, where he remembered Borges, or the Mystic River, which reminded him of Clint Eastwood; he didn't think of Newbury Street cafés; he didn't think of Nadia, a little Russian with whom he flirted; he wasn't thinking of the old house across from the big Borders bookstore where the Boston Tea Party started; he wasn't thinking of the red facades of those beautiful Boston streets made for walking in the evening; no, his thoughts took him to one afternoon at the end of August, to a lunch with Helen in a restaurant at Boston College—in a cafeteria, actually—but only if the word "cafeteria" could refer to an eating place with good food. The lunch there was excellent. At the very end, Helen's colleague, a history professor, joined them for lunch. He said his name was Larry. Helen introduced the Writer, adding that he was from Bosnia. The Writer was used to the fact that the only association Americans had with his homeland was war and Sarajevo, but Larry wasn't like that. In those fifteen minutes of conversation at the table Larry mentioned Andrić and Tito, Turkey and Austria, Jajce and Travnik, Rebecca West and Arthur Evans. Helen had later said that Larry was interested in Eastern Europe professionally. Before his departure for the airport the Writer had made the last stop at the bookstore, even though he barely had any money left. His backpack was already full of books previously purchased, but he went in once more just for the sake of it. On one shelf in the corner he found a book he simply had to buy: Larry's book on Eastern Europe. The book flew over the Atlantic at the top of the backpack. Upon his return, the Writer put the book on the shelf without ever opening it. He often remembered a certain book he had bought and never opened, but would soon forget about it. It happens to everyone who loves books. But now, something, probably the memory of his meeting with Larry, prompted him to look for the forgotten book. After ten minutes of searching he found the yellow-gray volume and started leafing through it, glancing over chapter names and illustrations. His next step was looking at the index. He wanted to know if Larry had written about Bosnia in more detail. His eyes first sought Belgrade, and then Bosnia a few lines later, and then came the shiver. Somewhere between Belgrade and Bosnia he saw Bošković, Ruggerio Guiseppe. The book referred to Bošković's journey from Istanbul to Poland in 1762. This is a sign, thought the Writer, this is my story: the poet of the eclipse travels through the darker side of Europe.

Three

Waltz with Reality was the title of a book by István Eörsi. The book stood on the Writer's shelf between Cortázar's *Tango of Return* and Kundera's *Farewell Waltz*. When the ringing of the telephone woke him the Writer immediately thought of Ruđer Bošković since he had spent the entire night reading about him. He probably dreamt about him too. After a brief conversation he remembered the title from the bright yellow covers of the Eörsi book: *Waltz with Reality*. They called him from the weekly paper for which he worked. A journalist and a photographer were going to the town the Writer had grown up in to research an article about the sex trade, prostitution, and trafficking. The editor figured they might need the help from someone who knew the area so he asked the Writer to accompany them. Being groggy and awakened so suddenly, the Writer agreed. As soon as he hung up he regretted agreeing, but was reluctant to invent excuses. It would just be a day trip to Lašva Valley, where he'd have this waltz with reality and that same night he'd get back to Bošković.

The photographer and journalist came to pick him up in half an hour. In the meantime the Writer managed to have breakfast and coffee. The photographer drove and the journalist sat in the front seat. The Writer took a seat in the back. During the first ten minutes, while the driver tried to beat the morning rush on the way out of Sarajevo, the Writer talked to the journalist about the text she was planning to write. Her responses were vague: I'll visit several nightclubs, try to talk with the women I find there and with people who live nearby. She already had a confession from a nineteen-year-old girl, a victim of human trafficking who had managed to escape from one such whorehouse in the Lašva Valley. She also had some data and a conversation with an authorized person from the police. She was only missing a report from the scene. The Writer nodded. He didn't really know why the editor had asked him to go along. He leaned his head on the window and tried to sleep. David Bowie was playing on the radio. The photographer and the journalist talked quietly.

The Writer managed to drop off to sleep for a while. He woke a little before the intersection at Lašva. The traffic mirror at the crossroads was broken. The driver muttered a few curses. It's always like that, he said. I have driven this way hundreds of times but I've only seen this mirror intact maybe twice. I'd prefer, he added, never to have seen it in one piece. I usually curse the government but this is really not the government's fault. The government put it there and these monkeys smash it. That's what our people are like, chimed in the journalist. Primitive. I also heard they steal the streetlamps and sell them for old steel. I understand those people, reacted the driver loudly. At least they get some benefit from doing that, they even earn a bit—kill an ox for a pound of meat, as the saying goes. These creeps, on the other hand, he shouted, smash the mirror out of pure nastiness. They get nothing out of it, yet each day someone might die as a result. When the driver calmed down the Writer said: we used to call that *špigle*. After a brief pause, he continued. As kids we'd smash the mirror and each would take the pieces of it, and those pieces we called *špigle*. We used to play with them, he added. We used them to blind each other by reflecting the Sun's rays. I doubt that today's kids care about *špigle*, muttered the driver. One shouldn't underestimate the magic of mirrors, added the Writer to himself.

We're close, the journalist said. Can you park a little further and walk back as you take pictures of the exterior? She turned to the Writer: we'll just go in as if we stopped by for a coffee. I will not introduce myself as a journalist before I get a feel for the atmosphere inside. She turned to the driver again: after you photograph everything from the outside, join us inside, but hide the camera.

Night Club Queen. There was a sign with big letters on the front of the new kitschy building. The building looked like a seaside bed and breakfast. Judging by the windows it was clear that the house was divided into as many rooms as possible. The parking lot in front of the building was almost completely empty. The Writer felt uneasy but he didn't want to let that show in front of the journalist. He opened the heavy door and they stepped into the wide, dark space. The windows were all dark. It looked as if they were in a tunnel, even during the day. Their eyes were just getting used to the dark. The place was almost empty. Three men sat at one of the tables in the corner. The Writer and the journalist took a seat at the table nearest the door. The music wasn't playing loudly. A young waiter came over. The Writer ordered a glass of whiskey. The journalist added: I'll have one as well. When the waiter came back with the tray, the photographer had just appeared in the doorway. You're off to a good start—immediately jumping to the hard stuff. I'll have what they're having, he said to the waiter as he was taking his seat. When the waiter moved away from their table the driver whispered: it's all photographed. His drink arrived quickly and they all clinked their glasses.

The journalist took out a cigarette and started searching her purse for a lighter. The Writer was just about to pull out his when another hand appeared with a gold-plated Zippo. The Writer looked up. A tall, muscular man was standing by their table. My respect, Ma'am, good day, Gentlemen, he said. Thank you, said the journalist, and the Writer mumbled something. How did those photos turn out, my friend? the man asked the

photographer. Who wants to know? asked the photographer. I
want to know, my friend. I own this club. You are Mr. Crnalić,
chimed in the journalist. Yes, honey, I'm Crni, what do you
need? he asked while fixing his eyes on hers. The journalist was
about to introduce herself when Crni quickly interrupted. I
know, honey, who you are, I know whom you work for, I know
why you came here, he said. I also know what that whore told
you, he continued, the whore fell in love with me and I'm a
married man, so when I refused her, she started spreading lies
about me. Even the police don't trust her, so now she goes to
the papers, he said staring into the journalist's face. She didn't
turn her head. You deny that you're involved in trafficking? she
asked. I don't know, honey, what that means, he responded. In
Italy, while in prison, I learned Italian, but I don't speak English.
You don't organize prostitution? You're not involved in the sex
trade? the journalist asked, returning the same look. I don't ban
my workers from falling in love, he said, they work and dance
the whole night, they need to relax and let go somehow. There's
no prostitution here, that's illegal, he said making no effort to
hide the irony. He sipped his drink while he talked. Could I
talk with one of the waitresses, asked the journalist. They are
sleeping now, they are tired, responded Crni with a grin. I always
have men work the first shift. He invited a waiter. Do you want
to talk to him, he asked. The journalist shook her head. Bring
them another round, Crni said to the waiter once he approached
the table. Don't include me, I'm driving. Come on, said Crni,
what are just two drinks for such a man. You didn't come all
the way from Sarajevo to have only one drink, he added. When
the waiter came back, the owner ordered him: go ahead and see
if Olga woke up, this journalist wants to talk to her. See what
kind of man I am? Let's agree on one thing, he continued, do
not take pictures of Olga. Fine—you photographed the club
from the outside, it's not an army building, but I won't allow any
picture-taking inside, he said while raising his voice and looking
at the photographer. Afterward he leaned toward the journalist

and said, Olga is Russian and she barely speaks Bosnian but you'll manage to communicate somehow. It's all poor folk over there in the Eastern Bloc. These girls come here to earn a few pennies. The journalists call them hookers, that's not nice, but you see for yourself. He finished and in one gulp drank all the remaining whiskey from his glass.

Just then the waiter showed up with a short blond girl in her late twenties. Here comes our little Olga, exclaimed Crni. Come on, girl, take a seat. Bring Olga a screwdriver; he added to the waiter, and for me and the gentleman, Crni pointed toward the Writer, one more whiskey each. These two drink slowly, he added, winking at the Writer in a somewhat conspiratorial manner. He finally turned to the girl. Listen, Olga, this lady wants to know if you're having a nice time here, she doesn't believe me, she wants you to tell her that, he said. He spoke slowly while Olga nodded. She looked at the journalist. It's great here, she said. How long have you been here, Olga? the journalist asked. Olga nodded again. Six month, she said, I be here, in this club. In Bosnia I be two years. Why did you come to Bosnia? asked the journalist. I work here, I'm a waitress, Olga said and blushed, or so the Writer imagined. What kind of education do you have? the journalist was interested. I studied Russian literature, Olga said. It tells you a lot about the situation in Russia, said Crni while getting up, when their literati are waiting tables. I'm going to the washroom, said the owner. You two talk a bit more, but not for a long time, Olga needs to rest, she's working tonight. As soon as the owner moved away, the journalist started speaking Russian, quickly and quietly. You know Russian? the Writer uttered, but she interrupted him with a gesture. Olga did not seem surprised. The journalist put a Dictaphone on the table. The two of them spoke for about two or three minutes before the photographer started coughing loudly. The journalist put the Dictaphone back in her purse and went back to speaking Bosnian. Are you planning to go back to Russia? she asked Olga. I would like to. When I save some money, said Olga. It's true, honey, you said it well, everyone misses their home, said Crni. I missed Bosnia when I was in Italy, especially when I was in prison. You should go now, Olga. Get some rest, he ordered her. Olga got up silently and moved away from the table with her head bowed.

Maybe it's time for you to go back to Sarajevo, said Crni after a short pause, that would be best. The Writer reached for his wallet. Never mind, man, I'll take care of this.

They left the place quietly and walked to the car. As soon as they got in the photographer turned on the radio. The voice of David Bowie accompanied them. They were quiet all the way to the intersection. What a character, said the Writer finally. You don't know anything, the journalist said. What did Olga say? the Writer asked. Horror, the journalist said, such a horror.

On the way back to Sarajevo the Writer listened to the story. It was worse than a nightmare. The journalist spoke quickly, retold the confession of the runaway nineteen-year-old girl, Olga's story. Crni currently has twenty female slaves, she said, the youngest one is sixteen, and the oldest is twenty-seven. They bribe the police with sex, she said. They're scared, crazed out of their minds, lost, and entirely powerless, she said. If a girl gets sick, they beat her up, if she complains, they beat her up, if she tries to complain to a customer, they beat her up, she said. If they try to escape, and they catch her, a long torture and death awaits her. That poor girl who managed to escape to Sarajevo, they all think she was slaughtered.

What will happen after your article? the Writer asked. What will happen? the journalist asked bitterly. Nothing. Even if there is some alert prosecutor and he sends the police they will pretend that nothing happened, let them screw some for free and they'll write up a report about Crni as a reputable club owner who respects the law.

It was crowded again at the outskirts of Sarajevo. They were all silent, only the driver swore a few times. They dropped the Writer off at the building entrance.

The Writer took a shower and changed when he got home. I'll pour a whiskey, he thought, and I'll write my story, the story of Bošković. He poured the whiskey, but his thoughts couldn't focus on what he wanted, they kept going back to Olga. She said she was from St. Petersburg, the Writer remembered, the same Petersburg to which Bošković was headed from Istanbul, the same Petersburg that Bošković never reached, the same Petersburg to which Olga wanted to return, but he was afraid she wouldn't.

Maybe this is my story, the Writer thought, the story about Olga, the story of that girl from Moldova who managed to escape hell, the girl whose name the journalist never uttered, the girl whose story was painful to listen to. While the journalist told her story, the Writer tried to concentrate on Bowie's voice, he wanted not to hear the horror, not to know about it. He looked at the green pastures and tree blossoms and scattered herds of sheep. He sang to himself, but he knew that the horror would enter his consciousness when he closed his eyes, in silence.

They headed to the West and South, reaching the light, the women and the girls, they were running away from the cold, from poverty, they followed the Sun. They didn't know anything about the Sun they were following. Ruđer Bošković knew. He knew about the eclipse of the Sun.

Four

18ᵗʰ of May

Birthday. Bošković's and mine. And Bertrand Russell's. By the way, Russell seems to have read Bošković. Some even think that Bošković's influence on Russell's thought is very significant. Lately I've been reading Russell. I'm jotting down a quotation from his book Religion and Science: *"From ancient times, comets had always been regarded as heralds of disaster. This view is taken for granted in Shakespeare, for example, in* Julius Caesar *and* Henry

V. *Calixtus III, who was Pope from 1455 to 1458, and was greatly perturbed by the Turkish capture of Constantinople, connected this disaster with the appearance of a great comet, and ordered days of prayer that "whatever calamity impended might be turned from the Christians against the Turks." And an addition was made to the litany: "From the Turk and the comet, good Lord, deliver us." I found the following sentence by Martin Luther while reading Russell, "The heathen write that the comet may arise from natural causes, but God creates not one that does not foretoken a sure calamity." Was Christ's birth a calamity, according to Luther? The star of Bethlehem often appears in the form of a comet, as in Giotto's painting. I read somewhere that the star of Bethlehem is actually Halley's Comet. In "The Comet" by Bruno Schulz I find an echo of an old prejudice that Russell talks about: "One could scarcely believe that that tiny maggot, shining innocently among the innumerable swarms of the stars, was Balthazar's fiery finger writing the destruction of our globe on the tablet of the sky." There is a fragment in Kiš's* Hourglass: *"Franz Joseph was then emperor. A war was going on in Bosnia and Herzegovina. There was a solar eclipse and a comet was sighted."*

8th of June
Maria is the most beautiful female name, in all its variants: Mary, Mashenyka, Merima. There isn't a male name as beautiful as Maria. As is the case with most beautiful rivers, the etymology of the name Maria is unknown. The root and the origin of its beauty cannot be found. Some say that Maria is a rebel, others that it means sea of bitterness, while some others claim that Maria stands for a well-fed woman. The name Maria always gives something secretive and special. In Springsteen's best songs the woman is always named Mary. Nabokov's first novel is named after its heroine Mashenyka (who becomes Mary in English translation). Andrić has Mary in his title "Mara Milosnica" (which sounds almost like Maria full of grace). Even Bazdulj has a story about a waitress from Bosnia named Merima who serves old Borges and Maria Kodam in Geneva.

14th of June

If Christ was welcomed to this world by a comet, it was the eclipse that saw him off. The evangelist Matthew recalls darkness that descended after the crucifixion. Was it an eclipse of the Sun on Good Friday? Astronomy says no. But on one April Friday in the year 33 an eclipse of the moon was seen in the sky above Jerusalem.

23rd of June

Midsummer's night. As Borges says, today the streets remember that they used to be fields. What was Bošković remembering on Midsummer night while he traveled to Poland? What was he dreaming of? He was most likely not dreaming about the fact that a hundred years later Nietzsche will refer to him as Pole. Nietzsche mentions Bošković in passing, as Auster mentions Tesla, as Thomas Pynchon mentions Bošković. Both Bošković and Tesla are people from the East. In the best case the West mentions them in passing.

3rd of July

I watched a video I Wish I Was a Punk Rocker. *The singer was a girl I just heard about today. I also saw her for the first time. The song is pretty. The girl is young, about twenty years old. She complains that she wasn't born at a time she could be a punk rocker with flowers in her hair. The verses describe such a time wonderfully: children playing outside, people writing letters to each other (the video even starts with a scene of someone throwing a letter into a mailbox), soccer players grow their hair long, people listen to records, and all in that style. But the most important part is in the refrain: revolution was hanging in the air. After that, the girl, Sandy Thom, sang: I was born too late in an indifferent world.*

I'm looking at Sandy. She is beautiful. Intelligent face, long dark hair, wearing a black retro jacket. This is how I imagine Maria. Maria's problem, however, was not that she was born too late, but too far to the East. Her problem was not that the world was indifferent, but that it was evil.

14th of July
Rebecca West calls Bošković "a wild Slav version of the French encyclopedists, a mystic, a mathematician and physicist, a poet, and diplomat." Nonetheless, unlike the texts of the French encyclopedists, Bošković's texts represent "hymns to science as an enlightenment of God's deeds." Yes, Bošković was a Jesuit. I graduated from a high school in Travnik that is still called Jesuit, even though the Jesuits haven't been in charge of it for the past fifty or sixty years. Andrić, in Ex Ponto, *writes about the Jesuits: "On one occasion I spent a day with two Jesuits. Peculiar people. They have a way about them by which they express their politeness that is somewhat disgusting. I was surprised by their sociability and vigor. They constrict conversation to a narrow, indifferent area, and strictly fence themselves off but give the illusion that they move freely. They laugh, joke, and have fun. I manage to forget myself and become interested until some gesture, or a look, or a pause, reminds me of something unpleasant." Dostoevsky's influence? In his novels it is an ultimate offence to say about someone that he is a Jesuit.*

20th of July
I'm reading Dostoevsky. Notes from the Underground. *The story about Liza reminds me an awful lot of the story about Olga from the Queen nightclub in Lašva Valley. It's a different epoch and different geopolitical factors. Liza is from Riga. She arrived in St. Petersburg. Riga and Latvia are no longer East or "stolen West." This is what the man from the underground tells the twenty-year-old prostitute: "You will leave everything here, everything, irreversibly, your health, youth, beauty, hope, and at twenty-two you'll look thirty-five, and pray to God not to get sick." When he talks about Petersburg's prostitutes, Krleža recalls Rebecca West: Slavic anarchy, Asiatic pessimism, tragic weight, laceration, and imbalance, and all of this because of the "hundred-year-old schism between East and West." The cause of the schism is historical: the East didn't have the rationalism of medieval scholastic philosophy or a renaissance.*

27th of July

Bošković did not get a chance to see Venus's transit over the Sun, the same way I didn't get to see the Eclipse. The first time he didn't make it to Istanbul, and the second time the Jesuit order did not allow him to travel to California despite an invitation by the Royal Society from London. Transit doesn't have the symbolic attraction in comparison to Comet and Eclipse (there was a transit a couple of years ago and people didn't make a big deal of it), but it was precisely the transit of Venus over the Sun, the one that Bošković did not observe from California, that was responsible for the discovery of Australia. The same Royal Society hired James Cook to observe the transit from the South Pacific. In the meanwhile he discovered Australia.

I am listening to Nick Cave. The album is No More Shall We Part. *Cave was born in Australia. He was married in the summer of 1999, on a day of a total eclipse of the Sun. I am listening to the song "Sorrowful Wife." The song begins with a verse: "I married my wife on the day of the eclipse."*

30th of July

Elizabeth Costello is Australian as well. I am reading her considerations of the notion of evil. I think she has the gist of it. There are writers, wonderful writers, Llosa and Sabato, for example, who describe unseen cruelty with precision and in great detail. I like Llosa, I like Sabato, but after reading those pages with the descriptions of atrocities, I always felt sick. I felt nauseous listening to the details of the confession by that unknown girl who finally ran away from the hell of forced prostitution. I felt nauseous when, during the war, the newspapers published descriptions of Chetnik crimes. I had a hard time fighting the nausea but I didn't want to analyze it. Now, however, Elizabeth Costello is helping me. Some things are, according to Elizabeth Costello, so horrible that they resist words. Nevertheless, the main argument concerns the word "obscene" and it goes like this: "Obscene. That is the word, a word, *a word of contested etymology, that she must hold on to as talisman. She chooses to believe that obscene means off-stage. To save our humanity, certain things that we may want to see (*may want to see because we are human!*) must remain off-stage." A few lines later the thesis is explicitly formulated: "... certain things are not good to read* or to write. *To put the point in another way: I take seriously the claim that the artist risks a great deal by venturing into forbidden places: risks, specifically, himself; risks, perhaps, all." In the story about a girl who followed the light one must not descend to complete darkness.*

One more thing: her examinations of the problem of evil Elizabeth Costello presents in Holland, "country of windmills and tulips"—as she calls it herself, country of Beatrice Porter, Bošković's fellow traveler on the journey from Istanbul to Poland.

5ᵗʰ of August
I'm reading Bošković's acquaintance from London, Samuel Johnson: "It is naturally indifferent to this race of men what entertainment they receive, so they are but entertained. They catch, with equal eagerness, at a moral lecture or the memoirs of a robber; a prediction of the appearance of a comet, or the calculation of the chances of a lottery." In the famous Johnson biography written by James Boswell, Bošković is described as a "celebrated foreigner" and the function of his appearance in this book is merely an opportunity to establish that Doctor Johnson spoke Latin very well and how a "celebrated foreigner" was delighted because of it.

11ᵗʰ of August
I heard of Moldova for the first time on Dynasty, *the TV show. The youngest daughter of the Carringtons, Amanda, marries a Moldovan prince. Some terrorists kill all the protagonists on the show. Later, the story about Sherlock Holmes and Doyle resurfaced; due to eager fans the producers revived the characters and the show continued. Moldova used to be, for both the screen players and directors, an ideal Ruritania—a non-existent country with a poetic*

name. The fact that Amanda's character was played by Catherine Oxenberg, an offspring of the Karadžordević dynasty, almost an exotic princess, gave the whole idea, or it may seem that way, a type of postmodern charm. Life may imitate art, but this is definitely a parody of soap opera. Moldovan daughters are nowadays taken by fake princes, and the country that was taken to one war by the Karadžordević was taken to another by the Carringtons.

15th of August
In the opinion of Slavoj Žižek the highest achievement of literary postmodernism is E. L. Doctorow's book Lives of the Poets. *He argues, "The charm of this book is that it gives us the opportunity to reconstruct the artistic process from the raw material of the writer's everyday life." The title reminded me of Suetonius, whom Bošković had read on his journey from Istanbul to Poland. Krleža notes about Suetonius that he was and remained "chronique scandaleuse; those are pornographic stories from the gentlemanly alcoves, motives of plots and gossip, but nevertheless, they were infinitely more credible than the official, apologetic, court historiographies." That was, I think, in the afterword to* Aretej. *That same afterword, that mutatis mutandis, tells me how to write about my own phantoms: "I know that both phantoms should be represented simultaneously, because neither one nor the other matters on its own. What matters is my own condition here, these long, horrible nights in these rooms, now, during the infinitely long nocturnos. Yet again, if both of these, so different, so separate, almost inconceivably remote phantoms were brought to the scene together with the whole overflow of its anxious motives and concerns, what could come of this verve?"*

17th of August
"The ability and willingness to associate everything I read with my own enthusiasm seems almost funny, if one were to observe oneself from the side, however, as due to some kinship, everything is a bit akin to and has some association, advancing on me from all sides." (Thomas Mann: Creation of Doctor Faustus*).*

Five

At the beginning of every September the Writer remembered the lines of Odysseas Elytis, the Greek Nobel Prize winner, that he had read long ago in an anthology of love poetry: the first drop of rain killed the summer. The days were still relatively long but the equinox was approaching. The Writer didn't like that time of year. The autumn melancholy was now intensified by his literary resignation. I know how to write, thought the Writer, I know what to write, but I don't know why to write.

As the residue of the books he had read, the Writer finally realized that his favorite authors considered literature unimportant. With Kiš, Andrić, Sartre, and many others he found an idea that was formulated to him through the words of Elizabeth Costello. Writing is like a genie in a bottle; when the storyteller opens the bottle, the genie is let out into the world, and perhaps it would be better if the spirit remained in the bottle—that is how the whole idea about the absurdity of writing rang in his head.

On those days the Writer stayed away from the keyboard. He didn't write for the papers, didn't use the Internet—nothing. He barely read. He listened to music, but mainly to two or three songs: Nick Cave's "The Kindness of Strangers," Bruce Springsteen's "Maria's Bed," and Leonard Cohen's "Chelsea Hotel." The films he saw were mostly made by Scandinavians: Lars von Trier, Thomas Vinterberg (with whom he shared his official birthday), and Lukas Moodysson. One night he watched *Fucking Åmål* and *Lilya 4-ever*. How could the same director possibly make these two movies? he wondered. How is it that a distance of a few hundred miles between East and West could be so vast as to divide the beauty of kissing between the two teenage girls and the sexual slavery of their contemporary? And yet it's the same world.

He didn't eat or sleep much those days and he drank more than usual. One morning, when he woke—it was already early afternoon—he was looking into the bathroom mirror and he recalled the famous sentence by Borges: Mirrors and copulation are abominable.

In the midst of this melancholy the Writer was invited to travel to France. The Writer generally avoided all possible seminars, study periods, and workshops, being led by the knowledge that there is no free lunch and by the physical discomfort he felt when standing in line for a visa. The trip to America a few years earlier was the exception that confirmed the rule.

The travel date was set for the beginning of November and the Writer was to stay in France for seven days. Maybe I could use a change, thought the Writer, so he agreed to go as a reporter for a cultural festival dedicated to Bosnia and Herzegovina. The French embassy was sponsoring several journalists who were accredited to report from the festival—the Writer being one of them—so the process of getting a visa was less humiliating.

For some reason the Writer was sure that the festival was taking place in Paris. That was his reason for going on this trip. The Writer didn't like to travel, but when he traveled he liked to go to places he associated with people and books he liked. He set off for Boston and Cambridge because of Borges, Emerson, Poe, and Auster's *The New York Trilogy*. (The final scene of the trilogy takes place in Boston, in a dilapidated four-story building at number nine, Columbus Square.) He wanted to go to Paris because of Kiš, Andrić, Milosz, Camus, Baudelaire, Henry Miller, Calvin, Auster, Ruđer Bošković. He was looking forward to Paris. This joy had the same effect on him that fairy tales usually do, or that words do, as singer Johnny Štulić would have it—it had quieted the melancholy.

The joy wasn't necessarily bringing back his belief in literature, but it made the loss of his belief less tragic.

At the beginning of October he rented a cottage in the

mountains for a few days. I need a change before Paris, he thought. The grass was dry and dark green; the forest was in the full range of warm colors; the sky was clear; the only thing that seemed threatening was the purple reflection above the conifer treetops at dusk. As he walked along the steep paths the Writer recalled a couple of lines by Camus, "Nature is always here. She opposes human madness with her quiet heavens and her reasons."

The return to the city was a return to human madness. The bird's song was replaced by political megaphones and instead of seeing the color of autumn leaves he was seeing election posters. The overall noise was unbearable. The joyful anticipation of his trip to Paris was now even greater.

Almost by accident, just five or six days before his trip, the Writer realized that the festival wasn't taking place in Paris but in Saint-Nazaire, a place called Saint-Nazaire, as an acquaintance told him. I might have heard of the place at one point, but I didn't know anything about it, thought the Writer. The information he gleaned from the Internet was not promising: a port on the Atlantic, about sixty thousand people, no places of interest. The joy over the trip dwindled at that moment. He was tempted to cancel the trip but the plane ticket was already bought, the room reserved, so it didn't make sense not to go. There is no free lunch, thought the Writer, no free lunch. He made himself go but decided to spend only a day or two in Saint-Nazaire following the festival events and then to skip over to Paris for three or four days, at his own expense, and return for the festival's closing.

The night before the trip the Writer had a terrible headache. Typical travel fever, he thought. When he was a student he used to get these headaches when he went to Travnik for a weekend and back to Sarajevo Monday morning. He barely slept that night. In the morning he explained his tiredness by his lack of sleep. He was exhausted in the airplane, and this feeling was greater than his admiration for Paris from a bird's-eye perspective. His exhaustion was even greater after they landed. A bus had been sent from Saint-Nazaire to pick them up. While the others rejoiced as if they were on a school trip, the Writer slept. When he arrived at his hotel room the Writer took a shower and felt much better. The hotel was near the coast and the windows overlooked the sea. He lit a cigarette by the window but didn't enjoy it.

In the evening the festival organizers planned a dinner for the festival participants. The wine was excellent. The burning in my cheeks must have been from the wine, thought the Writer as he walked back to the hotel.

The next morning he woke up with a fever. He knew this feeling well. He checked his pulse: over a hundred beats a minute. He went downstairs for breakfast. He ate a bit of bread and had some tea. His body was shivering in the chair. One of the reporters from Sarajevo had brought medicine with her. She went to her room and brought a Tylenol. The Writer took two tablets and went back to bed.

The fever lasted for five days. On the first day the festival organizers sent a doctor to examine him, but she didn't tell him anything new: he had the flu, needed to sleep, rest, and everything would be fine.

The colleagues from Sarajevo kept their eyes on him. They stopped by once or twice a day to see him, brought him a thermos with tea, juice, oranges, and asked whether he needed anything. The Writer came down for breakfast every morning and that was the only time he left his room.

He thought about Ruđer Bošković and the young, unfortunate Moldovan girl by the name of Maria Alexandra. He thought of Bošković's sick days in Poland and Maria Alexandra's being in love.

He brought a few books with him from Sarajevo but he didn't have time to read. The TV was on. He mainly watched MTV. He didn't hear Sandi Thom during those five days, but heard a song by another sweet girl, Katie Melua. The song was about nine million bicycles in Beijing, about twelve billion light-years, about six billion people on Earth and about one special person.

The mention of light-years reminded him of Bošković, and the mention of a special person—of Maria Alexandra.

He felt worst on the fourth day. Even after a few cups of tea and several pills he didn't sweat enough, the temperature wasn't coming down. During the fever his thoughts were confused as if in a recollection of dreams. The features of Sandi Thom and Katie Melua synced into one—the face of Maria Alexandra. The darkness of the Queen nightclub turned into the darkness of the eclipse. The light of a cigarette thrown from the window was a comet. Everything merged: the Charles and Mystic Rivers with the waters of the Lašva, the mysterious river of his childhood; the transit of trafficked women and the transit of Venus over the Sun; Dubrovnik's view of the sea of his birth and the image of the sea he sees out his window. He sees a ship and it seems that this is the only ship in the world, the ship of ships, a ship in comparison to which all other ships are simply children's toys, pale symbols, a ship that goes to other shores, to the other side.

The next day the fever held, and a day later he felt he was getting better. That morning he didn't come back to his room after breakfast. He walked through Saint-Nazaire, he participated in the closing of the festival, and even ate at the farewell dinner. The next day they all took a bus to the airport and went back to Sarajevo.

I saw Paris from the air, and I only remember a few images from Saint-Nazaire, as if from Zoograf's comic strips. I traveled in vain, the Writer thought when he came back to Sarajevo. I didn't see Paris but my joy came back, thought the Writer when he woke up the next morning. He didn't feel like writing but he wanted to read. He searched his shelves for an unread book. He picked Nabokov's *Other Shores*. The Writer had bought that book long ago. As a student he found Nabokov's collected works in a used bookstore and read them all in one summer. Later he bought a few of Nabokov's books in English that weren't included in the collected works. Among them was Nabokov's autobiography *Speak, Memory*. He hadn't read it yet. When the

Writer was in Belgrade a few years ago he found *Other Shores*, a translation of the Russian version of Nabokov's autobiography, but he hadn't read this volume either until this morning. He read the book in one breath. As he was reading the next-to-last page the Writer experienced a shudder similar to a feverish shiver. The book was ending with Nabokov's family's departure to America. The port from which they sailed into new life was Saint-Nazaire. Nabokov's little son was a six-year-old and he saw there a "prototype of all the various toy vessels he had doddled about in his bath." The Writer recalled Mehmedinović's attitude toward writing: writing makes sense only if it is an excuse for the last sentence. The last sentence of Nabokov's book voices the following (and the Writer read it with a celebratory note): what is once seen cannot be unseen.

The thought had returned to him from almost twenty years back when the Writer was in the eighth grade. A kid from Nova Varoš had come to his class. He and the Writer were friends for a few months before the boy moved somewhere else. One evening, on their way back from school, the friend had asked the Writer the following riddle: If a man in a desert, he asked, at the moment of death, has a unique thought, so unique that it had never occurred to anyone before, and if that man does not write it down or doesn't say it to anyone, is such a thought forever lost? The Writer didn't say anything. His childhood friend was quiet for a moment but soon responded that the thought would not be lost because God would see it.

The Writer hadn't thought about this riddle in a long time. He didn't believe in God, but he believed that the thought, somehow, would not be lost. He recalled his favorite line by Johnny Štulić: "Don't worry, someone remembers every moment in a year."

He had seen Ruđer Bošković and Maria Alexandra. What is once seen can never be unseen.

He saw Ruđer Bošković examining mirrors at the fair in Karnobat. He saw little Maria Alexandra playing with her mirror. He saw them and their reflections in mirrors. As he sat down at his computer the Writer saw a reflection of his own face on the tinted screen.

On the ninth of November, at six fifty-three p.m., the Writer turned his computer on and started to write the story.

Muharem Bazdulj (1977) is one of the leading writers to emerge from the Balkans after the disintegration of Yugoslavia. His essays and short stories have appeared in twenty languages. Two of his previous books were published in English: *The Second Book* (2005) and *Byron and the Beauty* (2016). His work has been featured in the anthologies *Best European Fiction 2012* and *The Wall in My Head*. Bazdulj is also a winner of three of the most prestigious journalistic awards in Bosnia and Serbia. After fifteen years in Sarajevo, he is currently living in Belgrade.

Nataša Milas is a scholar of Russian and South Slavic literature and film, and a translator from Bosnian, Croatian, and Serbian. Nataša was a guest editor of the journal *Absinthe: New European Writing* with a spotlight on Bosnia. Nataša's essays and translations have been published in *Slavic and East European Journal, In Contrast: Croatian Film Today, In Translation, Brooklyn Rail, Absinthe,* and *Kino Kultura*. She lives in New York City.

MICHAL AJVAZ, *The Golden Age.*
The Other City.
PIERRE ALBERT-BIROT, *Grabinoulor.*
YUZ ALESHKOVSKY, *Kangaroo.*
SVETLANA ALEXIEVICH, *Voices from Chernobyl.*
FELIPE ALFAU, *Chromos.*
Locos.
JOAO ALMINO, *Enigmas of Spring.*
IVAN ÂNGELO, *The Celebration.*
The Tower of Glass.
ANTÓNIO LOBO ANTUNES, *Knowledge of Hell.*
The Splendor of Portugal.
ALAIN ARIAS-MISSON, *Theatre of Incest.*
JOHN ASHBERY & JAMES SCHUYLER, *A Nest of Ninnies.*
GABRIELA AVIGUR-ROTEM, *Heatwave and Crazy Birds.*
DJUNA BARNES, *Ladies Almanack.*
Ryder.
JOHN BARTH, *Letters.*
Sabbatical.
Collected Stories.
DONALD BARTHELME, *The King.*
Paradise.
SVETISLAV BASARA, *Chinese Letter.*
Fata Morgana.
In Search of the Grail.
MIQUEL BAUÇÀ, *The Siege in the Room.*
RENÉ BELLETTO, *Dying.*
MAREK BIENCZYK, *Transparency.*
ANDREI BITOV, *Pushkin House.*
ANDREJ BLATNIK, *You Do Understand.*
Law of Desire.
LOUIS PAUL BOON, *Chapel Road.*
My Little War.
Summer in Termuren.
ROGER BOYLAN, *Killoyle.*
IGNÁCIO DE LOYOLA BRANDÃO, *Anonymous Celebrity.*
Zero.
BRIGID BROPHY, *In Transit.*
The Prancing Novelist.

GABRIELLE BURTON, *Heartbreak Hotel.*
MICHEL BUTOR, *Degrees.*
Mobile.
G. CABRERA INFANTE, *Infante's Inferno.*
Three Trapped Tigers.
JULIETA CAMPOS, *The Fear of Losing Eurydice.*
ANNE CARSON, *Eros the Bittersweet.*
ORLY CASTEL-BLOOM, *Dolly City.*
LOUIS-FERDINAND CÉLINE, *North.*
Conversations with Professor Y.
London Bridge.
HUGO CHARTERIS, *The Tide Is Right.*
ERIC CHEVILLARD, *Demolishing Nisard.*
The Author and Me.
MARC CHOLODENKO, *Mordechai Schamz.*
EMILY HOLMES COLEMAN, *The Shutter of Snow.*
ERIC CHEVILLARD, *The Author and Me.*
LUIS CHITARRONI, *The No Variations.*
CH'OE YUN, *Mannequin.*
ROBERT COOVER, *A Night at the Movies.*
STANLEY CRAWFORD, *Log of the S.S. The Mrs Unguentine.*
Some Instructions to My Wife.
RALPH CUSACK, *Cadenza.*
NICHOLAS DELBANCO, *Sherbrookes.*
The Count of Concord.
NIGEL DENNIS, *Cards of Identity.*
PETER DIMOCK, *A Short Rhetoric for Leaving the Family.*
ARIEL DORFMAN, *Konfidenz.*
COLEMAN DOWELL, *Island People.*
Too Much Flesh and Jabez.
RIKKI DUCORNET, *Phosphor in Dreamland.*
The Complete Butcher's Tales.
RIKKI DUCORNET (cont.), *The Jade Cabinet.*
The Fountains of Neptune.
WILLIAM EASTLAKE, *Castle Keep.*
Lyric of the Circle Heart.
JEAN ECHENOZ, *Chopin's Move.*

FOR A FULL LIST OF PUBLICATIONS, VISIT: www.dalkeyarchive.com

STANLEY ELKIN, *A Bad Man.*
The Dick Gibson Show.
The Franchiser.
FRANÇOIS EMMANUEL, *Invitation to a Voyage.*
SALVADOR ESPRIU, *Ariadne in the Grotesque Labyrinth.*
LESLIE A. FIEDLER, *Love and Death in the American Novel.*
JUAN FILLOY, *Op Oloop.*
GUSTAVE FLAUBERT, *Bouvard and Pécuchet.*
JON FOSSE, *Aliss at the Fire.*
Melancholy.
Trilogy.
FORD MADOX FORD, *The March of Literature.*
MAX FRISCH, *I'm Not Stiller.*
Man in the Holocene.
CARLOS FUENTES, *Christopher Unborn.*
Distant Relations.
Terra Nostra.
Where the Air Is Clear.
Nietzsche on His Balcony.
WILLIAM GADDIS, JR., *The Recognitions.*
JR.
JANICE GALLOWAY, *Foreign Parts.*
The Trick Is to Keep Breathing.
WILLIAM H. GASS, *Life Sentences.*
The Tunnel.
The World Within the Word.
Willie Masters' Lonesome Wife.
GÉRARD GAVARRY, *Hoppla! 1 2 3.*
ETIENNE GILSON, *The Arts of the Beautiful.*
Forms and Substances in the Arts.
C. S. GISCOMBE, *Giscome Road.*
Here.
DOUGLAS GLOVER, *Bad News of the Heart.*
WITOLD GOMBROWICZ, *A Kind of Testament.*
PAULO EMÍLIO SALES GOMES, *P's Three Women.*
GEORGI GOSPODINOV, *Natural Novel.*

JUAN GOYTISOLO, *Juan the Landless.*
Makbara.
Marks of Identity.
JACK GREEN, *Fire the Bastards!*
JIŘÍ GRUŠA, *The Questionnaire.*
MELA HARTWIG, *Am I a Redundant Human Being?*
JOHN HAWKES, *The Passion Artist.*
Whistlejacket.
ELIZABETH HEIGHWAY, ED., *Contemporary Georgian Fiction.*
AIDAN HIGGINS, *Balcony of Europe.*
Blind Man's Bluff.
Bornholm Night-Ferry.
Langrishe, Go Down.
Scenes from a Receding Past.
ALDOUS HUXLEY, *Antic Hay.*
Point Counter Point.
Those Barren Leaves.
Time Must Have a Stop.
JANG JUNG-IL, *When Adam Opens His Eyes*
DRAGO JANČAR, *The Tree with No Name.*
I Saw Her That Night.
Galley Slave.
MIKHEIL JAVAKHISHVILI, *Kvachi.*
GERT JONKE, *The Distant Sound.*
Homage to Czerny.
The System of Vienna.
JACQUES JOUET, *Mountain R.*
Savage.
Upstaged.
JUNG YOUNG-MOON, *A Contrived World.*
MIEKO KANAI, *The Word Book.*
YORAM KANIUK, *Life on Sandpaper.*
ZURAB KARUMIDZE, *Dagny.*
PABLO KATCHADJIAN, *What to Do.*
JOHN KELLY, *From Out of the City.*
HUGH KENNER, *Flaubert, Joyce and Beckett: The Stoic Comedians.*
Joyce's Voices.
DANILO KIŠ, *The Attic.*
The Lute and the Scars.
Psalm 44.
A Tomb for Boris Davidovich.
ANITA KONKKA, *A Fool's Paradise.*

GEORGE KONRÁD, *The City Builder.*

TADEUSZ KONWICKI, *A Minor Apocalypse.*

The Polish Complex.

ELAINE KRAF, *The Princess of 72nd Street.*

JIM KRUSOE, *Iceland.*

AYSE KULIN, *Farewell: A Mansion in Occupied Istanbul.*

EMILIO LASCANO TEGUI, *On Elegance While Sleeping.*

ERIC LAURRENT, *Do Not Touch.*

VIOLETTE LEDUC, *La Bâtarde.*

LEE KI-HO, *At Least We Can Apologize.*

EDOUARD LEVÉ, *Autoportrait.*

Suicide.

MARIO LEVI, *Istanbul Was a Fairy Tale.*

DEBORAH LEVY, *Billy and Girl.*

JOSÉ LEZAMA LIMA, *Paradiso.*

OSMAN LINS, *Avalovara.*

The Queen of the Prisons of Greece.

ALF MACLOCHLAINN, *Out of Focus.*

Past Habitual.

RON LOEWINSOHN, *Magnetic Field(s).*

YURI LOTMAN, *Non-Memoirs.*

D. KEITH MANO, *Take Five.*

MINA LOY, *Stories and Essays of Mina Loy.*

MICHELINE AHARONIAN MARCOM, *The Mirror in the Well.*

BEN MARCUS, *The Age of Wire and String.*

WALLACE MARKFIELD, *Teitlebaum's Window.*

To an Early Grave.

DAVID MARKSON, *Reader's Block.*

Wittgenstein's Mistress.

CAROLE MASO, *AVA.*

HISAKI MATSUURA, *Triangle.*

LADISLAV MATEJKA & KRYSTYNA POMORSKA, EDS., *Readings in Russian Poetics: Formalist & Structuralist Views.*

HARRY MATHEWS, *Cigarettes.*

The Conversions.

The Human Country.

The Journalist.

My Life in CIA.

Singular Pleasures.

The Sinking of the Odradek.

Stadium.

Tlooth.

JOSEPH MCELROY, *Night Soul and Other Stories.*

ABDELWAHAB MEDDEB, *Talismano.*

GERHARD MEIER, *Isle of the Dead.*

HERMAN MELVILLE, *The Confidence-Man.*

AMANDA MICHALOPOULOU, *I'd Like.*

STEVEN MILLHAUSER, *The Barnum Museum.*

In the Penny Arcade.

RALPH J. MILLS, JR., *Essays on Poetry.*

CHRISTINE MONTALBETTI, *The Origin of Man.*

Western.

NICHOLAS MOSLEY, *Accident.*

Assassins.

Catastrophe Practice.

Hopeful Monsters.

Imago Bird.

Natalie Natalia.

Serpent.

WARREN MOTTE, *Fiction Now: The French Novel in the 21st Century.*

Oulipo: A Primer of Potential Literature.

GERALD MURNANE, *Barley Patch.*

Inland.

YVES NAVARRE, *Our Share of Time.*

Sweet Tooth.

DOROTHY NELSON, *In Night's City.*

Tar and Feathers.

WILFRIDO D. NOLLEDO, *But for the Lovers.*

BORIS A. NOVAK, *The Master of Insomnia.*

FLANN O'BRIEN, *At Swim-Two-Birds.*

The Best of Myles.

The Dalkey Archive.

The Hard Life.

The Poor Mouth.

The Third Policeman.

CLAUDE OLLIER, *The Mise-en-Scène.*

Wert and the Life Without End.

PATRIK OUŘEDNÍK, *Europeana.*
The Opportune Moment, 1855.
BORIS PAHOR, *Necropolis.*
FERNANDO DEL PASO, *News from the Empire.*
Palinuro of Mexico.
ROBERT PINGET, *The Inquisitory.*
Mahu or The Material.
Trio.
MANUEL PUIG, *Betrayed by Rita Hayworth.*
The Buenos Aires Affair.
Heartbreak Tango.
RAYMOND QUENEAU, *The Last Days.*
Odile.
Pierrot Mon Ami.
Saint Glinglin.
ANN QUIN, *Berg.*
Passages.
Three.
Tripticks.
ISHMAEL REED, *The Free-Lance Pallbearers.*
The Last Days of Louisiana Red.
Ishmael Reed: The Plays.
Juice!
The Terrible Threes.
The Terrible Twos.
Yellow Back Radio Broke-Down.
RAINER MARIA RILKE, *The Notebooks of Malte Laurids Brigge.*
JULIÁN RÍOS, *The House of Ulysses.*
Larva: A Midsummer Night's Babel.
Poundemonium.
ALAIN ROBBE-GRILLET, *Project for a Revolution in New York.*
A Sentimental Novel.
AUGUSTO ROA BASTOS, *I the Supreme.*
DANIËL ROBBERECHTS, *Arriving in Avignon.*
JEAN ROLIN, *The Explosion of the Radiator Hose.*
OLIVIER ROLIN, *Hotel Crystal.*
ALIX CLEO ROUBAUD, *Alix's Journal.*
JACQUES ROUBAUD, *The Form of a City Changes Faster, Alas, Than the Human Heart.*

The Great Fire of London.
Hortense in Exile.
Hortense Is Abducted.
Mathematics: The Plurality of Worlds of Lewis.
Some Thing Black.
RAYMOND ROUSSEL, *Impressions of Africa.*
VEDRANA RUDAN, *Night.*
GERMAN SADULAEV, *The Maya Pill.*
TOMAŽ ŠALAMUN, *Soy Realidad.*
LYDIE SALVAYRE, *The Company of Ghosts.*
LUIS RAFAEL SÁNCHEZ, *Macho Camacho's Beat.*
SEVERO SARDUY, *Cobra & Maitreya.*
NATHALIE SARRAUTE, *Do You Hear Them?*
Martereau.
The Planetarium.
STIG SÆTERBAKKEN, *Siamese.*
Self-Control.
Through the Night.
ARNO SCHMIDT, *Collected Novellas.*
Collected Stories.
Nobodaddy's Children.
Two Novels.
ASAF SCHURR, *Motti.*
GAIL SCOTT, *My Paris.*
JUNE AKERS SEESE, *Is This What Other Women Feel Too?*
BERNARD SHARE, *Inish.*
Transit.
VIKTOR SHKLOVSKY, *Bowstring.*
Literature and Cinematography.
Theory of Prose.
Third Factory.
Zoo, or Letters Not about Love.
PIERRE SINIAC, *The Collaborators.*
KJERSTI A. SKOMSVOLD, *The Faster I Walk, the Smaller I Am.*
JOSEF ŠKVORECKÝ, *The Engineer of Human Souls.*
GILBERT SORRENTINO, *Aberration of Starlight.*
Blue Pastoral.
Crystal Vision.

Imaginative Qualities of Actual Things.
Mulligan Stew.
Red the Fiend.
Steelwork.
Under the Shadow.
ANDRZEJ STASIUK, *Dukla.*
Fado.
GERTRUDE STEIN, *The Making of
Americans.*
A Novel of Thank You.
PIOTR SZEWC, *Annihilation.*
GONÇALO M. TAVARES, *A Man: Klaus
Klump.*
Jerusalem.
Learning to Pray in the Age of Technique.
LUCIAN DAN TEODOROVICI,
Our Circus Presents...
NIKANOR TERATOLOGEN, *Assisted
Living.*
STEFAN THEMERSON, *Hobson's Island.*
The Mystery of the Sardine.
Tom Harris.
JOHN TOOMEY, *Sleepwalker.*
Huddleston Road.
Slipping.
DUMITRU TSEPENEAG, *Hotel Europa.*
The Necessary Marriage.
Pigeon Post.
Vain Art of the Fugue.
La Belle Roumaine.
Waiting: Stories.
ESTHER TUSQUETS, *Stranded.*
DUBRAVKA UGRESIC, *Lend Me Your
Character.*
Thank You for Not Reading.
TOR ULVEN, *Replacement.*
MATI UNT, *Brecht at Night.*
Diary of a Blood Donor.
Things in the Night.
ÁLVARO URIBE & OLIVIA SEARS, EDS.,
Best of Contemporary Mexican Fiction.
ELOY URROZ, *Friction.*
The Obstacles.
LUISA VALENZUELA, *Dark Desires and
the Others.*
He Who Searches.

PAUL VERHAEGHEN, *Omega Minor.*
BORIS VIAN, *Heartsnatcher.*
TOOMAS VINT, *An Unending Landscape.*
ORNELA VORPSI, *The Country Where No
One Ever Dies.*
AUSTRYN WAINHOUSE, *Hedyphagetica.*
MARKUS WERNER, *Cold Shoulder.*
Zundel's Exit.
CURTIS WHITE, *The Idea of Home.*
Memories of My Father Watching TV.
Requiem.
DIANE WILLIAMS,
Excitability: Selected Stories.
DOUGLAS WOOLF, *Wall to Wall.*
Ya! & John-Juan.
JAY WRIGHT, *Polynomials and Pollen.*
The Presentable Art of Reading Absence.
PHILIP WYLIE, *Generation of Vipers.*
MARGUERITE YOUNG, *Angel in the
Forest.*
Miss MacIntosh, My Darling.
REYOUNG, *Unbabbling.*
ZORAN ŽIVKOVIĆ , *Hidden Camera.*
LOUIS ZUKOFSKY, *Collected Fiction.*
VITOMIL ZUPAN, *Minuet for Guitar.*
SCOTT ZWIREN, *God Head.*

AND MORE ...